Madeline Maguire had a preoccupation.

Spike was coming to the party tonight.

"Looking for someone?"

Mad glanced over her shoulder at her friend Sean. She smiled, and lied to one of her nearest and dearest. "I'm not looking for anyone. Not at all."

Unfortunately, Madeline *was* interested in Spike. But like most men, Spike didn't say much while he was around her and he didn't make a lot of eye contact. Yet when the door to the penthouse opened, Mad still flushed from her earlobes to her toes.

His big body filled the doorway. The hall. The whole apartment, as far as she was concerned.

Mad swallowed. It was not possible for a man to be sexier.

Dear Reader,

I have to say I loved writing about Spike Moriarty and Madeline Maguire! Spike took my heart the minute he walked into the books of THE MOOREHOUSE LEGACY, but I thought, who could possibly be a match for him? He's so outrageous and then…well, there's his very difficult past. But lo and behold, in came Madeline…strong, athletic, independent Madeline. I adored her from the get-go and knew without a doubt that she and Spike would have something special together. What a distance they had to travel, though, so many ups and downs…but that is often the course of love!

I hope you enjoy reading their book as much as I enjoyed writing it—and watch for Sean O'Banyon! His story, and those of his brothers, Billy and Mac, are up next. As always, I would love to hear from you. E-mail me at jessica@jessicabird.com.

Happy reading!

Jessica Bird

A MAN
IN A MILLION

JESSICA BIRD

Published by Silhouette Books

America's Publisher of Contemporary Romance

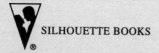 SILHOUETTE BOOKS

ISBN-13: 978-0-373-24803-2
ISBN-10:   0-373-24803-2

A MAN IN A MILLION

This edition published by arrangement with Harlequin Books S.A.

® and TM are trademarks of Harlequin Books S.A., used under license. Trademarks indicated with ® are registered in the United States Patent and Trademark Office, the Canadian Trade Marks Office and in other countries.

Visit Silhouette Books at www.eHarlequin.com

Printed in U.S.A.

Books by Jessica Bird

Silhouette Special Edition

Beauty and the Black Sheep #1698
His Comfort and Joy #1732
From the First #1750
A Man in a Million #1803

*The Moorehouse Legacy

JESSICA BIRD

graduated from college with a double major in history and art history, concentrating in the medieval period. This meant she was great at discussing anything that happened before the sixteenth century, but she wasn't all that employable in the real world. In order to support herself, she went to law school and worked in Boston in health care administration for many years.

She now lives in the South with her husband and her beloved golden retriever. As a writer, her commute is a heck of a lot better than it was as a lawyer, and she's thrilled that her professional wardrobe includes slippers and sweatpants. She likes to write love stories that feature strong, independent heroines and complex, alpha male heroes. Visit her Web site at www.JessicaBird.com and e-mail her at Jessica@JessicaBird.com.

With love to the better half of WriterDog.

Chapter One

Spike Moriarty raced down Park Avenue, legs pumping, arms swinging, black leather jacket flapping behind him in the night air. Big, in great shape and properly motivated, he was like an SUV tooling down the sidewalk. Oncoming pedestrians got out of the way.

Damn, he was *late*.

And this was no fifteen minute, margin-of-error kind of thing. This was a two-hour black hole of social impropriety.

Usually the rules and regulations of polite behavior weren't high on his priority list. He never went out of his way to offend people, but he wasn't in bed with Emily Post, either. But tonight was different. Two of his favorite people were getting married and this was their engagement party. He was supposed to be helping the host and giving a little speech.

Sean O'Banyon, master of ceremonies, was going to kill

him. Good thing they were buddies. It might buy him a quick and easy end.

Although it wasn't as if he'd been dogging it on his couch. The drive from upstate New York to Manhattan had taken twice as long as it should have on account of a fiesta of automotive trouble.

The kickoff had been an eighteen wheeler jackknifing on the Northway right in front of him. Fortunately, no one had been injured, but the semi fell over onto its side and shut down the southbound lanes entirely. Like everyone else, he'd been diverted to Route 9 and had become tangled in rural traffic.

Tangled, that was, until he got nailed by an eighty-five-year-old man driving an ancient Pontiac. Then he'd been stopped dead in the road. Thank God only the Honda had been hurt, but then the real fun and games had begun.

Local cops showed up. The pair of them took one look at Spike's hair and his tattoos and ran everything but his jockey shorts through every criminal check they could find. They probably even called Interpol overseas. The two had seemed bitterly disappointed when they'd found no outstanding warrants or parole violations. And to work off the frustration at not getting to use the cuffs, they'd detained him at the side of the road for about two hours.

By the time Spike finally made it back onto a highway, he knew he could kiss off any hope of making it to the party before the speeches started. Hell, he'd be lucky if he made it before folks left. After dropping a voice mail message at Sean's, he'd had to resist the urge to red line the Honda's speedometer. What stopped him was knowing that the last thing he needed was another run in with some badges.

Once he'd made it to the city, he'd dumped the car in a

lot and started hightailing it. For the middle of May, the night was blessedly cool and clear so at least he wasn't going to look like a total mess when he arrived.

Spike glanced at a street sign. *Thank God.* Only a couple more blocks to go. If he made good time, he figured he'd get to Sean's before Alex and Cass—

The taxi came out of nowhere. One minute Spike was shooting across 71st Street, the next he was looking the grill of a yellow Chevrolet right in the teeth. Years of physical conditioning gave him the reflexes and strength to yank his six-foot-four body out of the way. But he did bounce off the car before ending up on his ass in the street.

The taxi skidded to a halt, and evidently the driver didn't appreciate the assault on his hood ornament. He flipped the bird and hit the gas, kicking up some loose stones that pinged off Spike's biker jacket.

Much as he could have used a breather, he didn't hang around resting on his laurels. One: there was no time, not even to swear a little. Two: the asphalt was hard. Three, and most important of all: he had on black clothes, because that's all he ever wore, so he was indistinguishable from the street. He probably looked like an odd-shaped pothole.

He bolted up and kept running, figuring he'd find out soon enough if anything hurt. When nothing howled, he went faster, letting the motion of his body clean any debris off his slacks.

Finally, he saw Sean's building up ahead. He shot under the red and tan awning, peeled back the glass door and headed right for the elevators.

As he punched the Up button, a nasal voice cracked through the marble lobby. "*Excuse* me?"

Spike turned around toward the receiving desk. The

doorman he knew wasn't on duty tonight. But Colonel Klink's evil twin was. The guy was a dead ringer for the *Hogan's Heroes* commandant, just without the monocle.

Wait, that was a double negative of sorts. Klink *was* a bad guy. So maybe this was his doppelganger?

Spike shook his head, wondering if he had brain fry. Between pants, he managed to get out, "I'm here for… O'Banyon's party. My name's…on the list."

Klink's eyebrows arched in a haughty rendition of *Yeah, right, loser.* "Bike messengers aren't allowed up in the building. You'll have to leave whatever you're delivering with me."

Oh, man…

Sometime soon this night was going to end, Spike thought. One way or another, it was going to be over.

Madeline Maguire hung around the fringes of the engagement party, thinking that she didn't really have her land legs yet. Or her interpersonal ones, either. As a professional sailor, she spent most of her life battling the ocean and it was always hard to downshift into some semblance of normalcy whenever she took a break.

So this kind of social playing field felt like Mars.

Part of the problem was a crushing lack of urgency. On a racing yacht, every word was significant, every creak a clue to be deciphered, every minute shift in direction an important event. As a result of years of experience and training, her instincts were finely tuned and hyperalert. And her capacity for multiprocessing what they told her was one of the reasons she was such a good navigator.

In this environment, however, there was absolutely nothing to respond to.

Which left her feeling flat.

The high point so far had been arriving and seeing Alex Moorehouse. Alex had been captain of the crew she'd belonged to and was not only her mentor but a friend. He and his fiancée, Cass, were two of the finest people Mad knew and seeing them was well worth the hassle of getting to Manhattan.

In fact, the whole crew had wanted to come tonight, but the rest of the boys were stuck in the Bahamas rehabbing a boat after a bad storm. Following an unanimous vote, Mad had been designated the official ambassador. It was a good choice and they all knew it. The boys didn't do the civilized world all that well and it was better for everyone that the representative from the crew be able to put up a good front.

Not that she was doing so well at the social stuff right now, Mad thought. She could make a wallflower look like a Dallas Cowboys cheerleader.

Except there was no one she really wanted to talk to. The fifty people in the penthouse were mostly from her half brother's world: powerful, edgy men with competition in their blood; willowy, beautiful women with hard eyes and harder smiles. Of course, not everyone was like that. Alex's family was warm and lovely and there were a few others who seemed approachable. But somehow, the players stood out and made her want to hang back.

Plus, she had a preoccupation.

Her eyes sifted through the party again, scanning faces and bodies, searching for a tall, broad-shouldered man with black hair that stood up in spikes.

Spike had to be coming tonight. Alex was one of his closest friends. And from what she'd heard, so was Sean.

He just had to be coming.

"Looking for someone?" a deep voice asked from behind her.

Mad glanced over her shoulder. Sean O'Banyon, Wall Street genius, mostly reformed street thug and all-around good guy, was giving her one of his *gotcha* stares.

She smiled. And lied to one of her nearest and dearest. "I'm not looking for anyone. Not at all."

"Come on, Mad. Your eyes are playing floor hockey with every man in here. Except you're not finding the one you want, are you? So who do you wish you were seeing?"

Sean was the brother she wished she had instead of the one she'd gotten. But she didn't feel comfortable talking about Spike with him. The two were friends. And besides, given her history, nothing good was going to come of whatever interest she had in the man.

And unfortunately, she *was* interested in Spike. She'd met him when she'd headed up to Saranac Lake this winter to see Alex. The attraction had been instantaneous on her end, but she'd kept it to herself. Like most men, Spike didn't say much while he was around her and he didn't make a lot of eye contact. And no touching, not even casually.

So it was pretty much what she was used to. When you were six feet tall in your stocking feet and a professional athlete, most men didn't think of you as girlfriend material. Or even as a female. If they liked you, or respected you, you were one of the guys. If they didn't, they stared at you as if you were an alien or wrote you off as a lesbian.

Usually, either reaction was tolerable to her. More than tolerable, really, considering her few tragic attempts to make a connection with someone of the opposite sex. It was just… She wanted Spike to notice her, and not as an oddity, but as someone he might like to put his arm around. As somebody he might want to kiss, even just once.

She winced, trying to think of the last time she'd had a man's lips against hers. God, how long… Whoa, that was not a good number. Too high for someone her age, way too high.

And that would be years, not months.

"Mad? Where've you gone?" Sean prompted.

She shook her head. "Sorry. So I like what you've done to the place."

The penthouse he'd bought last year was done up fit to kill in a sleek, masculine style. Clean lines everywhere, minimal clutter, a lot of leather and metal. The panoramic views of the park and city were phenomenal and unimpeded by fussy drapes.

Sean glanced around. "Thanks, I like it. *Architectural Digest* photographed everything for next month's issue. Blair Sanford did the interior."

"It suits you."

"Yeah?"

"You're all about hard edges."

Sean laughed, his harsh face softening a little. "In my business, soft gets you spread like paste."

Sean had been her family's investment banker for the last ten years and he'd helped turn Value Shop Supermarkets into a nationwide chain. Her relationship with him, though, wasn't based on what he could do for her portfolio. She loved and trusted him more than she did her immediate relatives.

It was ironic. Usually she avoided men who looked like him because they reminded her of her late father and very-much-alive half brother. Sean had a real slick, glossy image. Dolled up in his fancy Savile Row suit and his silk tie, he seemed like your typical Wall Street money man. Except he wasn't. He'd grown up in South Boston, in a tough neighborhood, and he'd never forgotten the lessons he'd learned on the street.

Which meant he was also a little scary. And gave her only more reason to love him.

"Listen, Mad, we need to talk."

She cringed. "I can tell by the sound of your voice—"

"It's about your half brother."

Her eyes left his. "I'm not going to see Richard, but you can give him a message for me. Tell him to stop calling. He's using up my voice mail space."

"Mad, this is important—"

Up ahead, the door to the penthouse opened.

And Mad flushed from her earlobes to her toenails.

Spike was wearing a black leather jacket, a black button-down and a pair of black slacks. His jet-black hair was sticking straight up off his head in all directions, but instead of looking unkempt, the jagged peaks emphasized the hard lines of his beautiful face. His big body filled the doorway. The hall. The whole apartment as far as she was concerned.

Oh, God, his eyes… Those incredible, impossibly yellow eyes were still hidden under heavy lids and thick lashes. And the tattoos… On either side of his neck, two elegant, curving designs marked his skin. In his left ear, he had a thick, silver piercing.

Mad swallowed. It was not possible for a man to be sexier. Otherwise the laws of physics would collapse and the earth would implode into a black hole.

And no, she didn't think that scenario was an exaggeration.

"Holy Moses," Sean said under his breath. "You've been

looking for Spike, haven't you! How long's this been going on? When did you meet him? And why the hell don't I know about this?"

Mad took a sip of her Chardonnay and tasted nothing whatsoever. "Shut up, Sean."

Spike had just about had it with the world as he walked into Sean's apartment. He'd been okay with the stream of bad luck until he'd faced off with the lobby tsar downstairs. Now he was spanking pissed as well as embarrassed about being late. And he was hungry.

So heaven help the next person who screwed with him.

He pulled off his jacket, put it in the hall closet and immediately searched for Sean's dark head in the crowd.

It took a second and a half to find his buddy. And as he saw who was standing next to the guy, Spike's heart pole-vaulted into his throat.

Oh, good Lord. *She* was here. Madeline Maguire was *here.* Standing right across the room. Breathing the same air he was.

Or rather, breathing what he *would* have been inhaling if his lungs hadn't frozen solid.

But he should have known she'd come. She was Alex's navigator, or had been before the man stopped captaining America's Cup boats. So of course she would be at the guy's engagement party.

He just wished he could have gotten himself ready. Prepared. Controlled.

Although that would have required a sedative. And a blindfold.

As far as he was concerned, Madeline Maguire defined female perfection. She was confident and smart and tall enough to nearly meet him in the eye. Her no-nonsense warmth was a total turn-on and the rest of her was just as enticing. She had thick, dark hair that fell to the middle of her back. Her sapphire-blue eyes were bright enough to qualify as spotlights. And her smile had enough voltage to shock him right into an idiot-coma.

Tonight, she was wearing a black knit dress with a high neck and her body was…

Yeah, it was still perfect.

And he knew exactly what her curves looked like. He'd seen them, up close and personal. The first time he'd met her, she'd come out of a bathroom wearing nothing but a sports bra and a pair of black panties. She'd walked up to him, like she wasn't the most gorgeous thing on the planet, and expected him to shake hands as if Amazonian goddesses talked to him every day.

Then she'd asked to see his tattoos. He'd just about passed out.

In fact, he was feeling light-headed right about now, too.

But maybe that was just hypoglycemia, he thought with optimism. The last time he'd eaten had been six hours ago.

Spike hitched up his slacks, tucked in his shirt and walked over to her and Sean, keeping a tight rein on his face. If he didn't watch it, he was liable to start grinning like an imbecile. And shuffling his feet.

Man, where the hell was his game when he needed it?

"Hey, big guy," he said to Sean. "Damn sorry about the slow-up. Did you get my message?"

As he and Sean clapped palms, he knew instantly something was up. His buddy's eyes were twinkling.

And Sean O'Banyon, better known to most as SOB, was not a twinkler.

Sean glanced to his left. "No problem. You've met Madeline Maguire, right?"

Sure have, Spike thought. Saw her last night in my dreams.

As he nodded, he allowed his eyes one quick glance in her direction. Oh…wow. Those lips of hers were so pink. And she wasn't wearing any makeup at all.

"Hi, Spike," she said.

That voice. Low, husky. As sexy as he remembered it. His skin tingled.

"Nice to see you, Madeline."

She didn't offer him her hand and he was glad. He'd already tried out the whole puddle thing in the middle of 71st Street and hadn't found the experience all that enriching. So melting in front of her wasn't something he needed to do for a variety of reasons.

"What's doing with the speeches?" he asked Sean. "Have I missed them entirely?"

"Sorry, buddy. Time's come and gone."

"I better go make my apologies. Know where the happy couple is?"

"In my study, I think. Alex insisted that Cass get off her feet and I think he installed her in a chair and ottoman back there. He says the doc's probably going to put her on bed rest until she delivers the baby. Have you eaten yet?"

"Nah. I'm starved."

"Say, Mad, why don't you show our boy where the eats are?"

"That's okay," Spike said quickly. "I'll find the food. Oh, listen, do you mind if I crash here tonight?"

Sean popped a grin, a big, wide one that pulled out his dimple.

Man, this was such trouble, Spike thought. SOB's

hazel eyes had that whole *oh, goody* thing going on. What was he up to?

Sean clapped him on the shoulder. "I think that would be a great idea, Spike. Absolutely perfect. Don't you, Mad?"

For some reason, Madeline was eyeing the guy like she wanted to nail him in the shin.

Spike frowned, wondering how close they were. And in what manner of closeness it might be. He thought about what little he knew of the woman. She came from big money, supermarket money. So maybe O'Banyon was an advisor to her or something.

Sean winked at Mad.

Yeah, or maybe it was something more personal.

From out of nowhere, a mighty testosterone surge knocked out Spike's frontal lobe and higher reasoning. He was struck by an urgent need to push his body in between them. And maybe drag that handsome, dimple-sporting, eye-twinkling Sean O'Banyon into the hall closet.

He'd look just perfect hanging next to Spike's biker jacket. In the dark. Away from Madeline. Winking at himself. The bastard.

With a groan, Spike threw a leash on his inner gorilla, pointing out that Sean was a friend. FRIEND.

But then Mad looked at the man like the two shared a secret. And Spike's core primate started to thump its chest.

Sean is lunch, the thing said. LUNCH.

Okay, it was now retreat time. If he stayed much longer, his personalities were going to start arguing with each other. Out loud.

"Excuse us," he murmured, turning away. "I mean, me."

Chapter Two

Mad watched Spike work his way through the crowd. People stepped aside for him, eyeing his looks with curiosity and a hint of wariness.

And in the case of the women, a good shot of blatant sensual appraisal.

But then he was the kind of man who made you think about making love. The way his big body moved with such power and grace told you he knew how to use those muscles and bones of his. In all kinds of different ways.

"So, Mad, what is going on with Spike? I've never seen you this entranced."

She glanced at Sean and dodged the question. "I thought I was staying here tonight?"

"You are."

"You have one guest room."

"With two beds in it. And you guys are grown-ups, at

least in theory. Shouldn't be a problem, right?" Sean's grin got wider, if that was possible. "And, you know, if you get cold at night, I'm sure Spike would—ow!"

Mad hesitated, and then gave him a second nuggie, in case the first one hadn't made a big enough impression.

"Don't you dare throw me at that man," she said tightly.

Sean kept smiling, even as he rubbed his upper arm. "Who's throwing? I'm not throwing. He needs a place to stay, so do you. *Copious* amounts of no throwing."

She closed her eyes, feeling as if her heart had turned into a fist. "Sean… I'm serious. I can't— Please don't embarrass me."

There was a pause and then a heavy arm came around her shoulders. "Hell, honey, I'm sorry. I'd never do that. Come here."

She let herself get pulled up against Sean's chest. As she took a deep breath, her eyes focused on the doorway Spike had disappeared through.

Sean stroked her back. "It's just… I'd like to see you with someone like him. He's a good man. I know him well. He comes down here all the time and we hang together."

"Yeah, well, in case you haven't noticed, he didn't even look in my direction. He has no interest in me whatsoever."

"That can change."

"Not with me, it can't."

Sean cursed. "That stuff with Amelia and your boyfriend, it doesn't mean—"

"I don't want to talk about my half sister. And it wasn't boyfriend, it was boyfriend*s*. She slept with two of them."

Another curse. "Do you want me to tell Spike to go somewhere else?"

She shook her head. "I'm fine spending the night in the same room with him. But it wouldn't surprise me if he decides to leave. Now, look, you need to get back to your guests, okay?"

"Why don't you come with me and have some food?"

"I'm not hungry," she replied, which was her automatic response whenever anyone asked her to eat. "But thanks. Go on...I'm just fine."

After Sean left, and for the rest of the party, Mad kept to herself. And watched Spike.

He'd struck her as a quiet person when she'd met him up at the lake, but tonight, he was a real charismatic crowd pleaser. He and Sean started trading stories in the living room and soon there was a crew of people around them. A crew with a lot of women in it.

Which made sense. Sean had always been a lady-killer and Spike evidently was one, too. He had this half-cocked grin he sported whenever he let a good one-liner fly, and like the other women, Mad felt her heart kick up a notch every time that wry smile came out.

As the knot of people around him laughed once again, she shook her head. Boy, she'd read him wrong. He wasn't an introvert at all.

He was also very secure in himself. He seemed singularly unimpressed by the guests at the party and there were some pretty famous people around. It wasn't that he was unfriendly, though. He smiled and talked, shook hands and clapped shoulders. He just didn't kiss up. No matter who was standing in front of him, he never lost the slightly aloof, mocking confidence that drew people to him.

And speaking of magnetic, two women in particular had cozied up to him. Both were blond and aristocratic-looking, and pretty soon, one had her arm around him while the other tried to sit in his lap.

Mad shook her head, telling herself she had no right to be jealous.

Abruptly, Spike roared with laughter, the sound rich and very male. And then his eyes shifted across the room. As he caught her staring, his face tightened and the smile dropped off his lips. When the blonde sitting beside him playfully swatted at his chest, he recovered quickly and grinned down at the woman.

Yup, this was it in a nutshell, Mad thought. The story of my life.

The only time she wasn't invisible to men was when she was giving them attention they didn't want.

Spike had been totally surprised to find Mad looking at him and the shock of meeting her eyes had cut off his train of thought. He managed to finish his story about the first fish he'd cleaned as a chef only because he'd told the thing so many times, it was rote.

No doubt Mad thought he was just a rowdy show-off. And as the people around him broke out into laughter, he thought she was probably right.

Mad, on the other hand, wasn't rowdy or a show-off. She stayed away from the crush of people, lingering near the bank of windows, beautiful and still as a piece of art. In her regal silence, she made him feel awkward and unworthy, as if his stories were pathetic rambles with predictable starts and flat endings.

But then a lot of men at the party seemed to feel the same way about her. Every single male in the place had admired her from afar and obviously lacked the courage to approach her. What they settled for was looking at her from the corner of their eyes, watching her, measuring her. He saw all the glances and noted each one of them with a curse.

He knew exactly what kind of thoughts were going through those minds of theirs. The sexual speculation. The awe. The intimidation.

Because that sticky morass was swimming in his own head.

There was just something so…unreachable about her. It was as if she had seen things and done things on the ocean that none of them had come close to on land. And the gap worked against the men, setting them apart as pasty versions of something she probably didn't want and definitely didn't need.

And her beauty was downright threatening. Anchored by the strength of her body and her smart, smart eyes, she turned the other women at the party into f-words.

Frail. Flighty. Forgettable.

Spike felt something hit his chest lightly. Paige Livingstone or Livingworth—or something equally WASPy—seemed disappointed he'd retreated into his head. As did her sister, Whitney, who had somehow wiggled her way onto his lap.

Spike set Whitney aside and smiled in an empty way the sisters didn't pick up on. An hour later, after the party had wound down, he showed them both the door even though they'd given him their number and plenty of come-hither-you-bad-boy looks. He just wasn't in the mood to be their savage conquest fantasy. He'd done that before and had never really gotten much out of it even though the women had seemed to enjoy the experience.

Man…it was crazy, but for some reason, the sweater-set, pearl-draped, scarf-wearing types just went nuts for guys who looked like him.

Well, nuts for one night. Or maybe two. Though never longer than that.

Which was fine with him. He wasn't looking for a relationship.

No, he'd given up on that a long time ago. With his past, he wasn't ever going to settle down. As soon as a woman knew what he'd done and where he'd gone, she'd bolt and he was sure of this because it had happened to him. Since full disclosure was a guaranteed exit door, and he couldn't stomach lying by omission, he was never going to be more than a short-term visitor in a woman's life.

And he really was cool with that. He was a survivor both by nature and experience so his prime directive was clear. If you can't change something, you adapt and move along.

As Spike shut the door on the two blondes, he took a deep breath. The penthouse was silent now and the lack of noise was a relief.

Except then he realized that Madeline had left and he'd never gotten a chance to say goodbye.

Maybe that was just as well. Usually he had a good rapport with women; he could charm the pants right off them if he wanted to. But with Mad, there was no way to fake the social fluff.

And besides, all things considered, he should be grateful. He sensed she was someone he could fall hard and sloppy for. And where would that land him?

Ah, yes. 71st Street. On his butt.

Sean came out of the kitchen, tie hanging loose, shirt unbuttoned at the collar. He had two cups of coffee in his hand and he held one out.

"Thought you might need a pick-me-up, too," the guy said in a curiously disgruntled tone.

Spike took what he was offered and they made a beeline for the living room.

"So I think Alex and Cass had a fine time," Spike said. "And they were really nice about my being late."

Sean grunted. "You certainly looked like you were enjoying yourself. The Livingston sisters were all over you."

"Yeah."

They sat down on plush leather sofas that faced the bank of windows. Outside, the city glowed on the opposite side of the dense black square of the park.

"Too bad you spent so much time with them," Sean muttered.

"Huh?"

"There were other women at the damn party, you know."

Spike frowned and was about to ask what was doing, when he heard something behind him. He glanced over his shoulder. There was someone coming down the hall from the other end of the penthouse. A straggler?

Madeline came into the room as if he'd conjured her up from his fantasies. Her hair was all over her shoulders, rich and glossy, as if she'd just brushed it. And she'd changed out of that lovely dress and was wearing a pair of men's boxers and a tank top.

The two didn't quite meet in the middle so her belly button showed.

Spike shifted in his seat as Sean smiled and said, "Hey, Mad. Coffee's in the kitchen."

"Thanks." She strolled into the other room.

Spike watched her go, his eyes latching on to the sway

of her hips. And the muscles of her thighs and calves. And all the smooth, tanned skin of her legs.

Then it hit him.

"Sean? Is she staying here?"

"Yup."

Spike put his cup down and pegged his hands into his knees. As he stood up, he was aware of a stinging suffocation.

"Where you going, my man?" Sean murmured, Boston accent coming out thickly.

"I better take off." No way in hell he could be in the same apartment while Sean and Mad were in bed. Together. Doing unspeakable, fabulous things to each others' bodies.

God, just the thought of them together made him nauseous.

"Sit down, Spike."

"Nah, you need some privacy. I'll see you later."

"Spike, sitcha-ass down. It's not like that with her, okay? You can relax."

Spike narrowed his eyes and wondered if he'd given anything away about his attraction to the woman. It wouldn't have been much if he had, but when it came to his friend, it wouldn't *have* to be a lot. The trouble with O'Banyon was the guy was flipping brilliant. Never missed a thing, especially when people were trying to hide their inner goodies.

Usually it was a point in the man's favor. Not tonight.

Sean's voice stayed level as he nodded to the sofa. "Sit."

Spike sank back down. And then another thought shot through his head. He tried to remember how many bedrooms the place had. Not enough.

He eyed the couch. Pushed at it with his hand.

Good to go, he thought, imagining himself stretched out with his head on one of the cushions.

"Don't even think about it," Sean said.

"What?"

"Sleeping out here. There are two perfectly good beds in that guest room and you guys are going in them. She's already said she has no problem with it."

Him and Madeline Maguire in the same room? Alone? For like, six, seven hours? He'd be lucky if he wasn't limping by the time it was morning. All the pent-up desire in his blood would probably turn him into a pretzel.

Abruptly, Sean snorted and stared over the brim of his cup. "Why'd you have to spend so much time with Paige and Whitney?"

"They're easy." Spike picked up his coffee again. "I mean, they're simple. You know, just two women. And why do you care?"

"You should have spent more time with Mad."

Spike narrowed his eyes on his friend once again. "Are you trying to set us up?"

"Yes, I am. So the least you can do is be a gentleman about it and try and kiss her after the lights go out."

Spike nearly spit out what was in his mouth. "What the hell—"

"It's obvious you're into her."

He coughed, trying to clear his windpipe. "How do you figure I like her? I didn't talk to her all night long."

"Precisely. She was the only woman you were not comfortable around. And that spells attraction, buddy. At least the way I see it."

"You are deranged."

"True. And I'm right, aren't I? You like her. And *like* her, like her. Not just like her."

Spike rolled his eyes. "Holy hell, I feel like I'm in elementary school with this conversation. Where's my lunch box?"

"Same place your head is at." Sean's voice dropped down low. "I have it on good authority she's into you."

"And this is because she didn't talk to me, either? Sean, buddy, stick to finance. You're a rotten social worker."

"No, she—"

At that moment, Mad came back into the room, sipping from a mug.

Sean put his coffee aside and clapped his hands on his thighs. "I'm turning into a pumpkin. 'Night, all."

As the man left, he shot Spike a *don't-you-dare-screw-this-up* look.

And then Spike was alone with Mad. She didn't look at him, just walked over to the windows and stared out at the city. Silence elongated until he wasn't sure whether they'd been in the room fifteen minutes or ten days.

Well, if this wasn't awkward.

Spike said quietly, "I don't want to crowd you tonight. I can crash on the couch."

She shrugged. "If you want to. But bear in mind, I sleep on a boat with twelve men on a regular basis. No amount of snoring is going to get my attention. I can sleep through anything."

God, the small of her back was beautiful. He wanted to press his lips to the indentation of her spine. Run his hands around to her flat stomach. Reach down and ever so gently stroke her thighs—

"Spike?"

"What?" He looked up, meeting her calm stare as she glanced over her shoulder.

"You just made a funny noise."

"Did I?"

"Sounded like a groan."

Well, at least that was better than a squeak of desperation. Much more manly.

Although when it came down to it, he was surprised she couldn't hear the roar of his blood as the stuff slammed into all kinds of extremities.

"Can I ask you a question?" she said.

"Go ahead."

"Your eyes. Are they real? I mean, they're contacts, right?"

Spike looked away. He knew his irises were a peculiar color, but they'd been that way since birth. And most women liked them…thought the yellow was unusual and attractive. She was the first to suggest they were a cosmovanity statement.

Which told him a lot about what she thought of him.

And as he abruptly wished his peepers were normal, like a brown or a green or a blue, he got frustrated with himself.

He punched his weight into his feet, standing up in a quick surge. "I'm going to head for the shower. And then I'm hitting the sack."

"Spike, I didn't mean to…" Her voice drifted off.

"You didn't mean to what?"

"Offend you. I've just never seen eyes like yours before."

He shrugged. "I know they're weird, but, whatever, nothing I can do about it. 'Night, Madeline."

He put his coffee cup into the kitchen sink and then went down the hallway to the guest room. When he stepped through the door and glanced around, he expected to find her stuff all over the place. It wasn't. There were no errant hairbrushes or perfume bottles or clothes or shoes dotting the dresser or the desk or the chaise lounge in the corner. All he saw was a black duffel bag at the foot of the bed on the left.

A sailor's neatness, he thought, wondering what her life must be like.

He took a quick shower and then hunted around the vanity for one of the spare toothbrushes he knew was in there. As he put a high gloss on his teeth, he wasn't looking forward to getting back into the clothes he'd worn all day long, but he'd left his stuff in his car.

And like naked was even an option in the hypothetical? Not a chance.

Spike went still. On the other side of the door, he could hear her moving around in the guest room. She was probably getting into bed right at this moment.

And wouldn't that be a picture. Her lithe body bending down to pull the blankets back. Those long legs sliding between cool sheets. Her hair spilling over the pillowcase in waves of deep brown and dark red.

Cursing, he rinsed his mouth out, stepped into his boxers and then pulled on his shirt. While he buttoned the thing up, he eyed his pants. Throwing those on seemed a little much so he folded them and left them on the edge of the tub.

As he swung open the door, he expected to find Mad propped up in one of the queen-size beds, reading and looking wonderful.

Instead, the lights were off. In the glow from the bathroom, he could see her curled on her side with the covers pulled up to her cheeks. And yes, her hair did spill over the pillowcase beautifully.

As he stared at her, he wondered what the auburn waves felt like. Soft, he thought. They would be soft and they would smell like the herbal shampoo she'd left in the shower.

For the first time since his life had changed twelve years ago, he truly mourned the normalcy he no longer had and would never find again.

He thought about the one time he'd tried to have a relationship with a woman. About two years after he'd rejoined real life, he'd found someone he liked enough to want to get to know better. Things had gone well until he'd sat her down and told her about what had happened. She'd said all the right things at the time and he'd hoped they might go on from there. But then she'd stopped returning his phone calls.

He'd understood and let her go.

Ever since then he'd kept himself apart, although he hadn't been celibate. He'd just done the one-night stand thing when he'd wanted a little company.

Madeline Maguire was not a one-nighter. She was the real deal. A smart, beautiful woman from a high-class family that had a Brinks truck worth of money in the bank. So even if she'd been attracted to him, and she wasn't, there was no way someone like her would want to be…well, with an ex-con like him.

Spike went over to the bed on the right and got in it. After arranging the pillows the way he liked them, he tried to convince his skin of two things. One, the fact that he was wearing boxers and a shirt to bed was no big deal even though he usually slept in the nude. And two, Madeline Maguire's hands would in fact not feel like heaven if they were applied liberally over every inch of his body.

He failed. Particularly at the latter.

And goodnight-in-hell, everything was an irritant. He shifted this way and that on the bed. Couldn't find any comfortable way to lay.

Ten minutes later, he sat up, unbuttoned the shirt and tossed it on the floor. As he slid back down, he heard a soft chuckle from the other bed.

"Was that the shirt or the boxers? Or both?" she asked.

He froze, wondering just how long he'd stood at the foot of her bed and stared at her. Did she know he'd done that? "I thought you said you could sleep through anything."

There was a pause. "I guess I was wrong."

Her sigh as she burrowed back into her pillow burned through him.

Spike closed his eyes, hoping that the "fake it till you make it" theory worked with sleep.

It didn't. He was wide awake. Just staring at the insides of his eyelids.

Happy place. He needed to go to his happy place. Okay…right. Happy place.

Didn't have one.

God, how much BS was that? Everyone had one. He just needed to picture somewhere he wanted to be.

So how about the bed next door? the gorilla inside him suggested.

"Spike?"

His lids flipped open. "Yeah?"

"I don't think your eyes are weird. I think they're the color of sunshine on the waves in the early morning. They have that same hypnotic, shimmering quality, too." She cleared her throat. "Anyway, just wanted you to know."

His breath left him in a silent stream.

Shimmering. Color of sunshine.

He wanted to tell her that he was glad she thought of his eyes like that. And point out that anytime she wanted to get hypnotized, he'd kill to be her swami of choice.

"Thanks," he said, turning his head so he could see her. "My dad's were the same. Or so my mom told me."

Mad rolled over toward him, tucking her hands under her chin. God, she looked adorable like that.

"What nationality was your father?"

"Don't know. I never met him and I never asked her. Probably some European flavor."

"Why didn't you…"

"Know him?"

"I'm sorry if I'm getting too personal."

"Nah, it's fine. Mom said he didn't stay long, but she loved him like no other. And everything worked out eventually. Right after I was born, she met a guy who she ended up marrying. He was good to her, good to me. Plus I got a half sister, Jaynie, out of the deal."

"Have you ever wanted to find your father?"

"Wouldn't know where to start and my life's okay the way it is. So, no. Besides, Mom's lived in the same town all her life. If the guy wanted to find her or me, he could."

Spike frowned, wondering how long it had been since he'd spoken about his family to anyone.

He shifted so he was laying on his stomach and couldn't see her. She didn't say anything further. Neither did he.

But it was a long, long while before he could fall asleep.

Chapter Three

When Mad woke up around six-thirty, the first thing she did was turn her head and look at the man in the bed next to hers.

Her breath caught.

Spike was on his stomach, facing away from her, and he'd kicked the blankets off of himself. All that covered him was a thin sheet that was threaded through his legs.

So she finally got to see his tattoos.

He had two of them on his strong back—well, one really, with two halves. It looked like medieval scrollwork; the design running up his spine until it split to go over his shoulder blades and around to the front of him. The tail ends of it must be what showed on his neck, she thought.

The artwork was beautiful. The effect…erotic. The dark lines flowing over his smooth skin made her want to touch him. With her hands. Her mouth.

And not just on his back. She wanted to know his whole body.

It was obvious he lifted weights regularly. Those broad shoulders were thick with muscle and so was the heavy arm he had curled up next to his head. His biceps were so well-defined she could see the vein that ran down the front of them.

Unexpectedly, he let out a groan and shifted on the bed. She tensed, ready to turn over and pretend she was asleep, but then he took a deep breath and seemed to settle. His rib cage contracted as he exhaled and he moved his head up and down a little on the pillow.

There was nothing she wanted to do more than cross the short aisle between their beds and lie down against him. She could wake him up slowly by nuzzling his neck, maybe. Or kissing the top of his shoulder.

Yeah, and then what?

She was a virgin, not a vamp. And a man like Spike was going to want someone who knew what they were doing.

He made the sound again, deep in his throat.

That wasn't a groan, she thought. More like a purr.

His legs moved, the sheet pulling at them, constraining him. He rolled over onto his back. As his arm flopped out across the bed, she looked at his wide chest and his washboard stomach. Not a spare ounce of fat on him. Just a whole lot of muscle on a big male body.

Boy, she wished she had more experience. But in her life, there had been only two men who she might have become totally intimate with. One she met as a sophomore in college and the other she got to know during the summer after she left school to race. In both cases, she'd thought she was in love and assumed she was loved in return.

Instead, the men had preferred her half sister. And proved it beyond a shadow of a doubt.

Shortly after the second time someone she cared about ended up in Amelia's bed, Mad had put her dating life on hiatus. For one thing, if she wanted to be respected in her sport, she couldn't be with any of the men on the sailing crews she worked on or any of her competitors, either. But more to the point, there had been no way in hell she was getting vulnerable again.

Her life had gone on. A couple of years had passed. And now she was on the verge of being twenty-five years old and she'd never made love all the way.

It hadn't seemed like a character defect. Until now.

Spike let out another low rumble and his hand fisted against the sheets. In a flowing arch, his body bowed off the bed as if he were rising up to receive something. Then his hips moved in a tight circle, grinding, surging. Her eyes drifted downward.

Good Lord. He had an…

Well, it was clear what he was dreaming about, at any rate. And wow, she really needed to leave the room.

Spike's hips stopped moving, but his legs scissored restlessly and his calves turned into knots. He threw his head back and bared his teeth, inhaling with a hiss. As his chest and thighs went through a wave of contractions, the muscles tightened and relaxed under his smooth skin.

He murmured something that sounded like, "More."

Oh, man, he was beautiful. All male. Sexually aroused. In the throes of passion.

For a moment, she imagined she had the guts it would take to wake him up with the kind of sensuous caresses he was clearly getting in his dream. Would he turn to her?

Probably. At least until he realized she wasn't the woman he was fantasizing about.

She wondered who was in his mind right now, who he imagined was pleasuring him so acutely.

Without any warning, his eyes flipped open and he looked right at her. The yellow of his irises was so bright against his long, black lashes, it was as if his stare glowed. And the heat in it was like being hit with a blowtorch.

Mad jerked back. Then blurted, "I'm sorry."

Because watching him seemed voyeuristic.

The sound of her voice seemed to confuse him. His black brows dipped low and his head went back and forth a couple of times. He mumbled something, closed his eyes and rolled away.

Mad left in a hurry. She used the bath down the hall and then went to the kitchen, relieved to find that Sean wasn't up yet; she was not feeling particularly coherent.

Sean's kitchen was all stainless steel and wrought iron, halfway between a professional setup and a neo-classical café. After sitting for a while at the table in the alcove, she went hunting for a bag of coffee. She was about to get some brewing when she heard a yawn.

"Hey, woman." Sean walked in wearing a pair of plaid boxers low on his hips and a New England Patriots T-shirt. His dark hair was a tousled mess and his beard had grown in a little. He looked like a frat boy in his early twenties, not the thirty-five-year old Wall Street powerhouse he was. "So how'd you sleep?"

Mad looked away, just in case her blush was noticeable. "Fine."

"Spike keep you up?" As if Sean hoped that was the case.

"No, and don't start, okay?"

Her friend nodded, clearly sensing she was in no mood to play. "You know, this is heaven. You and my coffeepot, sharing a meaningful moment. Just beautiful."

"What have you got for breakfast around here?" She always kept her meals light and was hoping he had some fruit she could slice up.

"I don't know. I never eat at home. But the caterers cooked out of this kitchen all afternoon yesterday so there's got to be something."

The two of them cracked open the refrigerator and stared into it. There were all sorts of things crammed in there, a dizzying array of gourmet leftovers. Too many to choose from.

"I know exactly what this calls for," Sean said. "Wait right here."

He disappeared and returned a little later. "Help is on the way."

"You ordered takeout breakfast?" she asked as she poured herself some coffee.

"Better."

"You ordered breakfast delivered."

"I ordered us a classically-trained French chef."

"And this paragon is where?"

"Right behind you," Spike said.

She wheeled around.

Her eyes did a quick head-to-toe on him, she couldn't help it. He'd shaved and had all his clothes back on, but she still saw him on that bed in those sheets. His chest. His ribbed belly. His strong arms—

She realized was staring. And figured she better say something.

"You...are a chef?"

A bland look crossed his face and he went to the fridge. "I'm more the hash-slinger type, is that it?"

"No, I—"

"So what do you feel like chewing on, SOB?" he asked Sean sharply.

Shoot, she'd offended him. But she'd just been surprised that he would do something so traditional and rule-based. It wasn't that she thought he didn't have the intelligence and discipline it took to become a chef.

But Sean answered his question before she could explain herself. "Surprise me, buddy. Work your magic. In the meantime, Mad, you and I need to talk. And I'm leaving to go to Japan for two months this morning so it's here and now."

"Sean—"

"Come on, we're going into the other room. And let's hurry up so we're not late for breakfast."

Mad looked across the kitchen. Spike was gathering eggs, some leafy stuff and a couple of cheeses from the fridge.

He shot her a level stare. "Don't worry. I'm not going to burn the place down without your supervision."

"I didn't mean that comment as you took it."

"Okay. My bad." He sounded bored. And as though even if she had wanted to insult him, he wouldn't have cared.

She gave up and followed Sean into the living room. Her friend didn't waste time with any preamble.

"You need to go see your brother, Mad, and you need to do it before you head back out to sea."

Oh, not this again, she thought.

"Mad?"

"Half brother," she muttered. "He's my half brother."

"Don't get huffy with me." Sean sat on a leather sofa

and pulled her down with him. "Look, I'm not just telling you this as your buddy. I'm giving you some free professional advice. Go see him. Now."

"Why? My shares in the company are the only thing that interest Richard. And he's got control of them as executor of my trust." Together she and her half siblings owned the biggest portion of Value Shop Supermarkets, one of the largest grocery store chains in the nation. The holdings were valued at an absurd figure that Mad didn't like to think about. It was just too much to comprehend.

"Mad, in another week and a half he doesn't have to be. You're going to be twenty-five. Your father's will stated that when you reached that age, you could assume control of your holdings provided you took certain affirmative steps to do so. Otherwise, the current arrangement with Richard in charge prevails. He would continue to vote your proxies at board meetings for the next five years."

She frowned as it dawned on her that she hadn't thought about her trust or the company in years. Shirking responsibility wasn't in her nature and it was damn unappealing that she had assets she was taking care of. But her racing had always been the most important thing.

Abruptly, she focused on Sean. "Why are you looking so tense?"

"Frankly, I'm walking a whole lot of ethical and legal lines right now."

"But you're our investment banker. You're supposed to advise us."

"I'm the corporation's investment banker. And the CEO of that corporation, namely your half brother, could argue that I'm undermining him by advocating that you establish some independent control over your block of shares."

She winced at the implications, not wanting to cause Sean problems. "Well, I'm glad you brought it up. But Richard... Richard is going to hate not being executor. He's going to—"

"You can stand up to him. I know you can."

She wasn't so sure about that, but Sean had a point and she was glad he had told her about the trust's provisions. Except what did she do now?

"Mad, I have a lawyer friend of mine I want you to go see. His name's Mick Rhodes. I've briefed him on the situation, and as soon as you pull the trigger on him, he'll have the necessary documents drafted. Then you go see Richard. I know he's going to be in Greenwich next weekend for Memorial Day. Go to him there rather than to his office and don't bring Mick with you. Richard will view it as an act of aggression if you show up with your attorney. You want to approach him as his sweet, younger sister and then at 9:00 a.m. on your birthday, Mick will go and file the papers and it will all be over."

"But do I have to go see Richard? Why can't a lawyer just take care of the whole thing?"

"You're going to have to deal with the man at some point, why wait? You might as well not have this hanging over your head. And don't worry, I've heard Amelia's out of the country until the middle of June. She won't be there."

Mad pictured her half brother. Richard was razor-sharp, mentally and verbally. And she was quite sure some kind of liquid disdain pumped through his veins instead of blood.

"Legally he can't stop me, right?"

"I don't believe so, but he'll probably file a motion to block the change by arguing against your fitness as executor."

Probably? Try definitely. Richard hated losing and he fought dirty. Always had.

"But Mad, Mick will know how to deal with that."

"All right…I'll go to the lawyer right away."

Sean pulled her into his arms. "It's going to be okay. And I promise you, Mick's the best. He'll eat your brother alive if he has to. And enjoy every single bite."

Mad grimaced and murmured, "Half brother."

They stayed together for a time, with her wishing all the while she was Sean's sister instead.

When they returned to the kitchen, Spike was working over the stove, spectacular smells wafting up from all the pans he had going. He didn't look over as she and Sean sat down, but a few minutes later, two plates appeared on the table. On them were perfect omelets that looked out-of-the-world delicious.

"Oh, man, this is some serious beautiful," Sean said, Boston accent resurfacing. It seemed to do that when he was either really angry or really at ease.

"Thank you," Mad said to Spike, hoping to catch his eye.

He nodded to her and went back to the stove, making an omelet for himself while he cleaned up. By the time he sat down, Sean had finished eating and she was disciplining herself not to finish what was on her plate.

"Best omelet I've ever had," Sean said, wiping his mouth with a linen napkin. "You wanna get married?"

Spike shot him that half-mast grin. "What kind of ring will you get me?"

"Cartier?"

"Try Harry Winston. Four carats, minimum. And I want baguettes."

"Hard bargain. Very hard bargain."

"Have you had my leg of lamb yet?"

Sean's fist hit the table. "Rotten scoundrel. Plying me with inducements."

"I make the mint jelly myself."

"Fine. But I want you in a dress. No bride of mine's walking down the aisle in combat boots."

The two of them kept up the bantering and she let their deep voices fade into the background.

She wasn't at all sure she could stand up to Richard. Her half brother excelled at making her feel small, and yes, she let him do it to her. The trouble was, whenever she was around him, she felt like the five-year-old he'd picked on and it was hard to remember she was a grown-up.

So maybe it was time to slay the dragon, she thought. She was a professional with her own life, an adult in the world who was doing well. And those shares were the only thing her father had ever given her except for some serious self-esteem issues. Even if Richard was a peach, she should be responsible for what was hers.

"You can't come with me, can you?" she asked Sean abruptly. "To Greenwich."

The men's conversation halted.

"No, I'm sorry. I can't."

She nodded. "I didn't think so. It's just… Even without the business stuff, a holiday weekend with my half brother is going to be grueling."

"What you need is an armed escort."

"Yeah." She smiled. "Someone big. And tough…"

"You thinking Robocop tough or Arnold tough?"

"Let's get into this decade, shall we? Think Wolverine."

"Arnold's better."

She smiled. "Are we talking T2 Arnold?"

"Of course. I wouldn't want to send you into the sunset with the mean one."

Mad laughed, wondering why Sean had never settled down. He was such a nice guy behind those chilly eyes. But every since she'd met him when he'd started working with Value Shop's management team ten years ago he'd always been single.

While Mad and Sean batted action heroes back and forth, Spike finished his omelet and wiped his mouth. He was stone tired, but very alert.

God, that dream.

Sometime early this morning, he'd had a powerhouse of a fantasy about Mad. They'd been on a beach and tangled in each other's bodies, kissing and stroking and moving. She had been the single most amazing woman he'd ever been with.

Which was not a surprise.

As he remembered where they had been and what they'd done in his mind, he had the odd sense that he was being assessed. He looked up.

Sean was staring at him and the man seemed very serious.

"What? You want another omelet?" Spike asked.

Sean looked across the table at Mad and cocked an eyebrow. She shook her head.

"Go on," Sean said softly.

"What?" Spike put his napkin down.

Sean nodded at Mad, as if urging her on. She cleared her throat.

"Ah, would you come with me?" she asked. "To my family's house for Memorial Day weekend? My half brother will be there and there are a couple of parties scheduled. You know, typical holiday stuff."

Spike frowned, thinking it was clear she wasn't looking forward to being with her relatives. So why would she want to add to the burden by bringing a stranger with her?

Then he thought of the way she'd looked him over when she'd heard he was a French chef. *Right,* he thought. What better way to get back at her high-flying family than to show up at the house with a roughneck like him?

Man, this shouldn't hurt as much as it did, he thought. It really shouldn't.

"Not my bag. Sorry."

Sean spoke up. "Come on, you're perfect hero material, buddy."

"She's looking for a freak, not a hero, aren't you Madeline." Spike heard a little gasp as he rose from the table, but he ignored the sound as he carried his plate to the sink. "And while I can't deny I look the part, she needs to find some other fringe element to use. Hey, maybe she could just buy a weirdo of her own. She's got the cash, I'm sure. And that way, all she has to do is let him out of the closet any time she wants to shake things up."

He thought he caught another soft inhale, but he didn't let it stop him on the way to the door.

"Have a safe trip to Japan, Sean. I'll call you. And thanks for the bed."

Spike grabbed his jacket out of the closet, slipped it on and got in the elevator. He was through the lobby and out on Park Avenue before he heard his name being shouted. He glanced behind him. Sean was jogging over the pavement in his bare feet. And he was pissed.

"What the *hell* did you do that for, Moriarty?" the man demanded, getting right up into Spike's face.

"You're kidding me, right?"

"Mad did not deserve that potshot."

"Oh, but it's okay for her to want to use me?"

"I want you to apologize."

"Fine. Tell her I'm sorry. Later, Sean." He turned away, only to find a meaty hand clamped on his forearm. He looked down and then met his friend in the eye. "Do us both a favor and let go, buddy."

Sean cursed, then dropped the hold and used his palm to rub his face. "Look, Spike, she didn't mean it like that."

"Just like she didn't mean that crack about me being a chef?"

"Of course she didn't—"

"Did you catch the look she gave me? She clearly thinks I'm beneath her. And while that happens to be true, I don't need to be reminded of the fact."

"God damn it… Why are you so touchy around her? You're not usually like this."

Spike shifted his weight from foot to foot and then made himself take a deep breath. His temples were pounding even though he'd only had one glass of vodka the night before.

"Look, just leave it, okay? But tell her I'm sorry if she's upset."

"I want you to go with her."

He shook his head. "'Scuse me, Sean, but have we been having two different conversations here? I've said I won't and I mean it."

"But you'd be perfect, and no, not to drive her half brother around the bend. It's just you don't give a crap about all that social stuff and you won't be offended by anything Richard says or does to you. And if you went, she wouldn't be alone."

"First of all, Madeline Maguire is not the kind of woman who needs support troops."

"When it comes to her family, she does."

"Secondly, why doesn't she call on one of her real friends?"

"She doesn't have any."

Spike opened his mouth, prepared to go on to his third point, when he actually heard what Sean said. "What?"

Sean threw up his hands. "Mad's... She keeps to herself and there are some damn good reasons why she doesn't trust people. The only folks she's at all close to are the members of the sailing crew she's on—"

"So why doesn't she ask one of them?"

"They're stuck repairing a boat in the Bahamas. Look, there's some bad stuff going on with her half brother that she's going to have to deal with. You'd be a great buffer. And maybe something will...happen between you and her."

"Whatever."

"She likes you. She told me so."

Spike looked at the sidewalk, unable to believe his friend. "Don't—"

"Go. Please."

"I can't."

"Yeah, you can."

"No, *I can't.*"

"If not for her, than as a favor to me? Come on, Spike, I've waited for years for that woman to notice a man. She *sees* you. Last night, she spent the whole party waiting for you to walk through the door. She's really—"

"Stop." God, something close to panic was fanning in his chest. He had to open his mouth to breathe. "Sean, I don't—"

"I know you like her—"

"Just...*stop it.*" His voice sounded choked, even to him, and Sean obviously thought the same thing because the guy shut up.

Spike rubbed his hair. "Ah, hell, buddy... You're right, I do like her. She is special. I would love to be with her. But even if she was attracted to me, and I don't think she is in spite of what you say, I'm not the kind of man she's going to want to be with or bring home."

"What a load of horse—" Sean ended the statement with a four-letter word. "I haven't known you very long, but you're one of my best friends. And I'm a damn good judge of character. So is Mad, by the way."

"Sean, listen to me. I'm not right for her."

"Why? Give me one damn good reason. And it better not be the tats on your neck because I know for a fact they turn women on."

Spike looked down at his combat boots. Took a deep breath. "You say you haven't known me long? Well, you also don't know a lot about me. I've got a heavy-duty past, O'Banyon."

"Like what?"

Spike exhaled on a shudder. God, was he really going to do this?

He locked stares with Sean.

Yeah, he thought, he really was.

"Five and a half years at Comstock for manslaughter. That's maximum-security prison, Sean, and I did the crime. I killed a man. I killed him with my bare hands and I went to prison for it."

As his friend's hazel eyes peeled wide open, Spike wanted to curse. Damn it, he didn't want to lose Sean over this, he really didn't. But it wasn't like you could soft-pedal what he'd done. A human life taken was a shocking thing, as it should be.

"That's some hard time," Sean murmured. "How old were you?"

"Twenty-four when I did what I did. Twenty-five when I went in."

"Would you do it again?"

"If the circumstances were the same? Yeah. I would."

There was a long pause. "What happened?"

"Someone was beating my sister with a baseball bat. While screaming that he loved her. It was her life or her abuser's. I picked her."

Sean's shoulders eased up. "I'm glad you told me. And not just because of Mad."

"So do you understand why I can't go with her? Why I couldn't pursue her even if she'd have me?"

"No, actually, I don't. I'm willing to bet that if you told—"

"Already tried that on a woman once. Most females don't feel comfortable around a killer and I can't blame them. What I did…it doesn't sit well with me, either."

"Mad's not most women."

Spike shrugged. "Maybe so. But I know for sure she could find someone better to help her out of this little family storm she's heading into."

"I think you underestimate her." Sean shook his head. "Still, it's your decision. And no, I won't tell her anything."

"Except that I'm sorry."

"Yeah, I'll do that."

There was another long silence between them. Spike could feel Sean searching his face and knew the guy was running through all the implications of what had been revealed. Someone like Sean O'Banyon, big, fancy, finance guru that he was, was not going to want to hang with a violent felon, not with the high profile the guy had.

"It's okay, Sean," Spike said softly. "I understand."

"Understand what?"

"No prejudice, man. You and I can just go our separate ways. I'll disappear quietly."

Sean's lips thinned as he glowered. "Let me get this straight. You think I'd dump your friendship because of this?"

"Why wouldn't you?"

"You're such a lunatic."

Before Spike could say another word, two meaty arms shot out and pulled him into a fierce hug. Sean clapped him on the back hard enough to make his molars sing and then let go.

"Here's the deal, Spike. I've got a juvenile record that has been thankfully buried somewhere in a courthouse back in South Boston. And I do business with white-collar thieves all the time. So no, I'm not punting on you because of this. Jeez, what kind of lightweight loser do you think I am?"

As Sean glared, Spike cleared his throat, choking down a wave of gratitude.

"We're solid, Spike. You and me are cool. Got it? *Got it?*"

"Yeah, all right," Spike said hoarsely. "Good deal."

Up in the penthouse, Mad took care of the remaining dishes and washed the pans. Then she went into the guest room.

The bed Spike had slept in was made up perfectly. The pillows were all arranged neatly. The duvet was square on the mattress and smoothed out. The sheets had been tucked in.

It was as if he'd never lain there.

She went over and sat on the chaise. She couldn't totally blame Spike for thinking what he had about the invitation. It had come from out of left field and they didn't really know each other. She just wished she'd had enough time to explain herself before he left.

And it also would have been nice if he'd had a little more faith that she wouldn't want to use him, or anybody else, like that.

God, what had made her think for even a second that he'd want to spend a long weekend with her?

Mad listened to the silence in the penthouse, hoping to hear a door open and shut. She really wished Sean wasn't outside on the street yelling at Spike right now. She'd tried to keep her friend from going after the poor guy, but you couldn't stop a freight train just by standing in front of it.

Suddenly tired, Mad glanced over at the bed she'd used. Maybe she should go back to sleep—

She frowned, noticing the strangest thing.

One of her pillows was at the foot of the mattress. As if someone had dropped it there.

It hadn't been her. When she'd slipped out of bed, everything had been pretty much in place. But why would Spike have moved it?

She got up and walked over to the pillow. When she picked it up, she caught a whiff of aftershave. As if the thing had been held against a man's cheek.

How odd.

She put it against the headboard and stretched out on the bed. As she smelled the masculine scent again, she took a deep breath.

And yearned for what she couldn't have.

Chapter Four

A week later, Mad decided that one nice thing about the ocean was you never had to deal with traffic. Especially not the Friday of Memorial Day weekend, getting out of Manhattan, parking-lot-on-a-highway variety.

She turned the AC up a little higher and eyed the shoulder with evil in her heart. Her Dodge Viper was small enough to fit on the asphalt strip between the steaming cars on the road and the scratchy grass that ran up to the guardrail.

Too bad she was a lawful citizen.

With a curse, she glanced at her watch. Quarter after six.

Which meant, twenty miles away at the Maguire family estate, her half brother had just given the nod for the hors d'oeuvres to be passed. Cocktail hour would be over at precisely seven o'clock and the guests would sit down for dinner. Dessert would be cleared at eight. Coffee, brandy and cigars for the men would be offered on the terrace thereafter. Everyone would be out of the house at nine sharp.

It had been her father's timetable and she knew without a doubt that Richard had adopted the same schedule now that he was in charge. Dinner parties weren't so much thrown in the Maguire family as dealt like cards.

She thought about calling ahead and telling Richard that she'd be late, but she didn't have a cell phone and she wouldn't have dialed his number even if she'd had one.

It was time to approach the start line with him. So she needed to get her head together. The way she looked at it, this weekend at home was her crucible. A three-day event marked with obstacles.

It made no sense that someone with her athletic accomplishments found it so difficult to stand up to her family. And she was surprised by how stressed out she was, but then it had been a long time since she'd dealt with them. Her job on the ocean had allowed her to put old problems on the back burner, taking her far away from any contact with Richard or Amelia, lulling her into the false sense that everything was fine....

Allowing her to run away and keep running, which was her first instinct when it came to conflict.

So it was good that this issue with her trust had come up. Sometimes you needed to be forced to slay your dragons.

And she wasn't really going in without back up, even if she was alone in the car. She had a great new lawyer, one she had absolute faith in. Mick Rhodes had been all business when she'd met him at his firm's office. He'd reviewed the trust documents she'd brought with her, told her exactly how he was going to proceed, and warned her about what Richard was likely to do in response.

Which apparently wasn't anything Rhodes was too worried about.

If she had any hesitation about her attorney at all, it was because clearly the only reason he was taking her on was that Sean had asked him to. Rhodes was a heavy hitter corporate litigator, not a private client T&E guy. And she knew this because while sitting in the man's waiting room, she'd read all about him in the newest issue of *Business Week*. He'd been on the cover.

Anyway, with Rhodes in her hip pocket, she felt like she was going into battle with a Sherman tank. And didn't that make her feel better about her odds.

Except… well, the trust was only part of it. She really did need to learn how to relate to Richard. They were tied together through her father, and though that man was dead, the web he'd spun remained in the business he'd started. As well as in the bad blood he'd left behind among his children.

Forty-five minutes later, she spotted the Greenwich exit on the highway. As she got off, she tried to remember when she'd last been to the family house. It hadn't been since her father had died. So that was four years? Five?

Richard was the one who'd inherited the place and she was willing to bet everything was exactly the same now that he was living there. Say what you would about her half brother, he'd always been a loyal child. Loyal to the point of obsession. The son had not so much admired the father as he had aspired to be the father.

So yes, everything was going to be as it had been.

Mad drove through the town proper, smiling at the shops she recognized, assessing the new ones that had cropped up. She had memories of visits to the ice cream shop and the stationery store and the fruit market. The trips had always been chaperoned by different people. The nanny. The housekeeper. The cook. And she'd love the excursions not just for the excitement of it all but because she'd been with kind people whose company she'd felt comfortable in.

Beyond the town center, she came up to a pair of stone pillars that were marked with brass plaques engraved with the name Maguire in Old English text. As she eased into the driveway and proceeded down the alley of trees, her hands tightened on the Viper's gearshift and steering wheel.

Relax, she told herself. Just relax… This is going to be fine. Because you're going to make it fine.

She forced herself to breathe and took refuge in the summer splendor that surrounded her. The canopy of maples overhead formed a verdant tunnel and the grass that flowed over the grounds was a smooth, liquid green. Waning sunlight trickled through the leaves and dotted the drive…until it seemed that gold coins had been tossed from the heavens and were still bouncing as they landed.

What a beautiful color, she thought. So yellow, so bright.

She pictured Spike's eyes and wanted to curse.

Thoughts of that man were always popping into her mind, usually when she least appreciated the shocking jolt. Like now. Or when she was trying to fall asleep.

Boy, she and Spike had really gotten off on the wrong foot, hadn't they? Their few interactions had had the rhythm of a skipped record, mostly jarring, bad interruptions of what two people should be like when they met up. If only they'd had a little more time.

Yeah, but then what? He was all about blondes like the Doublemint twins and she didn't have a lot of chewing gum in her.

And yet…even though it was crazy, she hoped she'd see

him again. Maybe at Alex and Cass's wedding? Assuming she could get to the ceremony given her sailing schedule?

Or maybe…not at all. Maybe she would never run into him again.

Somehow that made her feel hollow.

Enough, she thought, taking the last bend in the drive. She had plenty to deal with considering she was about to take Richard by the horns. For her to waste time pining after some man was not only pathetic, but draining.

Mad eased up on the accelerator.

Up ahead, the house she'd spent her childhood in appeared before her like a mountain, all red bricks and white columns and black shutters. The place was a real show-stopper: twenty-one rooms on five acres smack dab in the middle of Greenwich.

The estate had been bought by their father when Value Shop Supermarkets had gone public in the seventies and it was just the kind of mansion you'd expect a business magnate to live in: big money even in a wealthy zip code.

Personally, she'd always liked the lawn best. It was great for catching fireflies and doing cartwheels. As for the rest of it—the pristine facade and the formal rooms and the decorator style and the antiques—that kind of stuff she could cheerfully leave at the side of the road. There was something about engineered beauty that made her nervous.

Probably because it was just such a cover-up in their case. Subterfuge for the ugly dysfunction within the family.

As she went around the circular drive, there were a number of cars parked in front of the house and not much room. She ended up easing the Viper in between a Mercedes the size of an elephant and a vintage, mouse-like MGB convertible. After turning off her car, she picked her duffel bag up from the passenger seat, got out, and realized she wasn't breathing again.

Looking to the sky, she wondered whether there was a patron saint for flinchy younger half sisters? Probably not.

So instead of praying, she decided to lead with the false confidence routine, squaring her shoulders and marching up to the house as though she had a backbone thick as a red oak.

The butler who answered the front door was someone she'd never seen before, but she recognized the formal dress. Her father had always made the staff wear uniforms and evidently so too did Richard.

"Yes?" the man said. His voice was as precise as his tidy gray hair. Matter of fact, he kind of looked like a living doll, all perfectly arranged. Eyes were even a little beady, too, though not unkind.

"I'm Richard's half sister, Madeline. Madeline Maguire." She felt like flashing a picture ID.

"Oh—ah, you are expected." Although clearly not what *he* had expected. "May I take your bag to your room?"

"Thanks. Are they already seated for dinner?"

"Yes." He hesitated as he took her bag. "But…perhaps you'd like to change before going in?"

"No." She was late enough already.

She thanked him again and went to face the lions. By the volume of talk coming out of the dining room, she figured there were probably twenty people tonight. Not a surprise. Her father had always said that was a good number. Intimate enough so there could be a single conversation over the table; public enough so that rivalries could be diffused.

The moment she came into the dining room's archway, Richard looked up from the head of the table. Somehow, it was a shock to seen him, even though he hadn't changed at all.

No, she thought, he was just the same. Still pale-haired, tanned, fit…with eyes like motion detectors. When Richard looked at you, you weren't so much stared at as surveilled.

While the conversation at the table dimmed, his eyes flicked over her, reviewing the khakis and the polo she had on. His annoyance and disgust were evident without the benefit of words: his lowered eyebrows said it all.

To avoid the urge to run back to her car, Mad assessed his guests. As she took in the group, all she could think of were salt-and-pepper shakers: everyone was lined up, men alternating with women, the whole lot of them glowing with wealth. And their fancy exteriors honestly seemed to house dry goods. Not a belly laugh in any of them, she'd wager.

"I'm sorry I'm late," she said to no one in particular.

"Traffic must have been awful," Richard replied smoothly. He nodded to an empty seat on his right. "You will sit here."

As several people murmured and all of them stared, Mad started on the walk of shame down the long, thin room, her loafers making a clicking sound on the inlaid floor. She smiled in a general way, feeling like an inept, ugly Miss America candidate. Who was about to get dinged by the judges.

When she sat down, Richard said under his breath, "You could have called."

"I know. But I don't have a cell phone."

"Which makes you the only person in America without one."

Richard turned away and promptly started to talk horses with the woman on his left, as if he were resuming a conversation that had been rudely interrupted.

Mad took a sip from her water glass and thought fondly of her new lawyer.

As a salad plate was put down in front of her, she snuck a peek at her half brother, and up this close, she realized he had in fact changed. Richard no longer resembled their father, he'd reached his life goal and had turned into the man: he was a carbon copy now, presiding over his fancy guests, eating with Christophe silver on Royal Crown Derby plates, sipping from Baccarat glasses. And yes, the Maguire family signet ring was on his right ring finger.

As their father had always worn it.

Looking at the stamp in the heavy gold, everything slid into place.

Richard was like a Brooks Brothers bobble head spitting back criticisms that had made her cringe when she was growing up: her father back from the dead. That was why she was so weak around her half brother. It wasn't just because he'd been hard on her when they'd been younger.

Putting a label on the dynamic kind of helped and she wondered why she hadn't figured it out sooner. Then again, she'd always done her best to avoid thinking about Richard.

Which was part of the problem, wasn't it?

Mad blotted her lips, returned the damask napkin to her lap and realized that she'd crossed her feet together under her chair like a good little girl.

Oh, hell, no, she thought. If she was going to make it through this weekend in one piece, she needed to fight the urge to fall into place.

Feeling like a rebel, she eased up, cocked one foot under her butt, and sat back down with her leg *on* the chair.

"Isn't that right, Madeline," Richard drawled.

"Excuse me?" She deliberately played with the tassel

on her loafer. Sure enough, Richard caught the movement and his eyes bugged out.

He opened his mouth as if he were going to scold her, but seemed to realize that would have been absurd.

As he cleared his throat, it seemed more curse than cough. "Penelope was commenting on the new Rubens exhibition at the Met. But I told her you wouldn't have seen it because that kind of thing doesn't interest you."

"Oh…well, I didn't know there was one." She'd always liked Rubens. His colors had such depth, it was as if you could dive into his paintings, swim in them. "I haven't been to the Met in a while."

"Penelope goes all the time. She's on the board." Richard smiled over at the woman and their eyes held.

Penelope was dressed in something white and expensive. And had about forty-five pounds of pearls around her throat, but no wedding ring. Maybe the two were a couple?

Richard lifted his wineglass. "Yes, I'm afraid the Met is of no interest to Madeline. She didn't make it through college and art seems to elude her. She likes boats."

"Boats." Penelope's drawn-on eyebrows arched. "How lovely." As if the interest were as inexplicable and unattractive as a flying pig.

Mad opened her mouth to try and do some damage control, but then shut it because she didn't really care what Penelope of the pearl noose thought of her.

She picked up her salad fork and—

From out of nowhere, a deep, throaty growl reverberated into the room. The bass throbbing grew louder and louder, until it cut off all conversation. Then it stopped altogether.

One of the guests laughed to fill the silence. "Maguire, old man, is Newcomb using your lawn as a landing pad?"

"That helicopter of his is horrid," a woman answered. "I mean, honestly."

Conversation lit up with a vengeance, a spark catching fire and blazing as the guests talked about whoever the "Newcomb nightmare" was.

Mad heard a knocking at the front door, but went back to poking the endive on her little plate. She was definitely not interested in any new arrivals.

Abruptly, the table went completely quiet again. And then the butler said, "Miss Madeline's guest is here."

Mad's head jerked up.

Spike was standing in the dining room's entryway, six feet four inches of raw man in black leather. He had a motorcycle helmet dangling from his hand, that infamous half smile on his face and his hair was a jagged crown. At his side, the butler looked kind of pasty and worried.

Mad was dimly aware of dropping her fork as Richard hissed, "Who the *hell* is that?"

Spike's yellow eyes scanned down the table until they found her. And his expression grew serious as he lifted his free hand in greeting.

"Spike!" one of the dinner guests exclaimed. "As I live and breathe!"

The man bolted up out of his chair and practically skipped his way around the table.

"Hey, Binder." Spike clapped palms with the guy.

Binder, whoever he was, kept a hold on Spike and looked at Richard with admiration. "You didn't tell me we were going to have a celebrity with us tonight."

"I wish I'd known," Richard muttered under his breath. Then he smiled. "Indulge me his credentials. As with all of my sister's friends, I've never met the man."

"This is one of *La Nuit's* greatest chefs. Worked with Nate Walker." There was a sudden chatter of approval from the guests and Binder went back to talking at Spike. "You two just opened a new restaurant in the Adirondacks. White Caps, right?"

"Good heavens," another man said. "I ate there last summer. Fabulous food. Fabulous!"

"And it was written up in the *Times,*" someone else cooed.

The room started buzzing as if Spike were a rock star. Which was good. Because Mad was still trying to catch up with the fact that the man had evidently come after her and she was so not up to fielding questions.

As Binder continued to chatter on, Spike took off his leather biker's jacket and tossed it casually to the butler. The other man sank from the weight of the thing.

When there was a break in Binder's fawning, the butler said to Spike, "Do you have…bags with you?"

"My stuff's on my Harley, but I'll get it later. Thanks."

Spike handed over his helmet and stalked down the length of the table, heading for Mad. Without skipping a beat, he picked up one of the chairs that was against the wall beside the sideboard and dropped the thing next to her, right on the corner. As he sat down, his big body blocked her view of Richard.

Spike looked at her, his gold eyes wary, but full of purpose.

"Hi, Mad," he said softly. "Hope you don't mind me crashing this shindig?"

Spike waited for Mad to respond. She was looking completely dazed, which was probably not a good thing. Ah, hell, he should have called.

"Excuse me, Madeline," the guy to Spike's left said.

"But perhaps you'd care to introduce me to the man you've invited to my house?"

Spike swiveled his head around. So this was Richard.

Man, no wonder she didn't want to come here alone. This guy was straight-up, high-class trouble, from his icy eyes to his signet ring to his perfectly turned-out bow tie. Real spit-and-polish nasty.

Mad cleared her throat. "I, ah, I wasn't sure he was—"

"My fault," Spike interjected. "I didn't let her know my other plans had changed. As you can imagine, I'm just thrilled to be here, Dick."

Richard's stare got transferred to Spike's face. "I go by Richard, thank you. And apparently, my guests think you're decent company. Which is a vote in your favor."

"Yeah, Binder and I go back." Spike smiled, showing all his teeth. "But I have to tell you, I'm not looking to get elected and I'm not here to be decent company. I'm here for Mad."

Richard frowned. "Indeed. And exactly how do you know each other?"

Spike glanced at Madeline, figuring this was a question she should answer.

"Friends," she said. "We're friends."

"That I could have guessed." Richard's voice was even. Well-modulated. Resonant. "Madeline doesn't have a lot of success with the opposite sex."

As Mad flinched, Spike narrowed his eyes. And wondered what good old Richard would sound like if his front teeth were knocked out.

But then he took a deep breath. Before he gave the tooth fairy some extra business, he should probably find out whether Mad wanted him to stay at all. He'd hoped to arrive after dinner so they could talk, but he'd been so anxious to see her that he'd left the Adirondacks too early and gotten to Greenwich too soon. And once he was in the vicinity, he hadn't been able to stay away from her house.

From across the table, Walter Binder spoke up. "So Spike, what are your long-term plans for White Caps? Are you going to expand? Maybe establish a presence in Manhattan?"

Spike cleared his throat to answer, but then had to lean back while silverware and a napkin and a glass were put down in front of him. The endive salad that landed in the middle of the setup looked good, but when the white wine bottle came forward, he shook his head.

"None for me, thanks," he told the waiter. Then he glanced over at Binder who, if memory served, was a deep-pockets real estate developer. "Ah, yeah…I think we do want to grow in the next couple of years. And though the Big Apple is a little far away from us, let's face it, New York is one of the hot spots for food in all the world."

"Are you looking for capital yet?"

"We're beginning to." As a matter of fact they'd already talked to Nate's brother, Jack, who had a pile of the stuff.

"Now that," Binder shook his forefinger in the air, "would be a great investment."

Talk shifted, moving in various wealth-related directions. As Richard launched into a conversation about the S&P with the anemic blonde next to him, Spike looked at Mad. Compared to the other guests, she was under-dressed in her white polo and her loose pants. But to him, she was absolutely stunning: all healthy and vital and beautiful. Man, Chanel had nothing on a pair of khakis when it came to Mad.

In a soft voice, he said, "I really should have called."

She pushed her endive around and smiled a little, the tilt

of her lips catching and holding his eyes. "I am a bit surprised to see you."

"I don't have to stay. I don't want to cause any problems for you."

She looked over at him, and suddenly, everything faded into nothingness. All he saw was the twilight color of her eyes, a blue so dark it seemed infinite.

The words came out of him quickly. "I'm sorry, Mad. About what I said back at Sean's."

"What? Oh...he told me you'd apologized. It's okay."

"No, it's really not."

Abruptly, Mad's eyes shifted to the left and she stiffened. Ah, so Richard was listening in.

"Let's go for a ride on my bike," Spike said quietly. "As soon as dinner's over."

She nodded. "I'd like that."

Spike picked up his fork, tucked into what was actually a very nice salad, and tried to stop staring at her. To distract himself, he surveyed the room and...*whoa*. He hadn't really noticed when he walked in, but the wealth and splendor of the environs was outrageous. If he'd been told the whole thing had been airlifted out of Versailles, he wouldn't have been at all surprised.

Funny, he'd thought he'd been ready to get a gander at her family's house. Even though he didn't come from anything, he knew a lot of rich people because rich people ate a lot of French food and they liked to know their chefs. But this...this was beyond rich and into Rockefeller money.

As Spike reached for his water glass, he knew that even if he hadn't had a prison record, Madeline Maguire was way outside his league.

Hell, he wasn't even from the same planet as her.

* * *

Mad put her spoon down, leaving the raspberry compote mostly untouched.

Food was *so* not on her mind right now. Probably because Spike Moriarty was taking up ninety-seven percent of her brain. With the remaining three percent seemingly focused on giving her hot flashes whenever her elbow touched his or their thighs brushed.

So actually, there wasn't anything left over, was there?

Which explained why she was breathless and there was a flutter in her chest. Clearly, her heart and lungs had gone free agent and without supervision, they were doing a rotten job.

The grandfather clock in the foyer began to chime.

"Let's have coffee on the terrace," Richard announced as he stood up. After he put his folded napkin next to his plate, he helped Penelope out of her chair.

Mad glanced over as Spike rose from the table. His leathers clung to his hips and his legs, the muscles underneath shifting and pulling at the second skin. She'd never actually seen a man wear something like that before. Had always assumed hardcore dressing was ridiculous, just a posing, calculation of masculinity.

On Spike, those pants were sexy as all get-out.

His big palm appeared in front of her. "You ready to ride?" His voice was low, naturally husky. "Mad?"

"Yes…I'm ready." She got up without accepting his hand, too flustered to touch him.

He dropped his arm. "Any idea where Jeeves put my helmet?"

"Leaving so soon?" Richard said. "Mad drive you away?"

"Hardly." Spike smiled easily enough, but his stare

had an edge like a dagger. "We're going to take a little joyride together."

"You'll miss the terrace."

"Guess so. But I have a feeling it will still be attached to the house when we get back." Spike smiled more widely, but only an idiot would have been fooled by the expression.

When her half brother frowned, Mad stepped in. "Spike, I think I know where your helmet is. Come with me."

"Sure. Love to. Later, Richard."

As they left, Richard's expression was along the lines of someone who'd just seen a UFO headline in the *New York Times*: utter disbelief tinted with dread.

Mad led Spike through the chatty throng of guests who were working their way out to the back of the house. Across the foyer and to the left, there was a hall closet and she opened it. As Spike reached up to get the helmet off the top shelf, he leaned into her, his big body brushing against hers, his aftershave a whiff of dark spice.

"Thanks," he said.

"Do you—ah, do you need your jacket, too?" She fingered its leather sleeve and resisted the urge to sniff the thing.

"Nah. It's warm and we won't be out long. I wore it for protection for the long trip. Just like these things." He casually slapped the outside of his thigh. "If I skid over asphalt, I'd rather all this leather need a skin graft instead of me, you know?"

Pictures of him in an accident made her panicky, reminding her that motorcycles could be dangerous even if the operator was highly competent.

"Mad? You okay?"

"Absolutely."

But as they went out through the front door, she was still a little shaken. At least until she saw what he rode.

She stopped dead. "Whoa. That is a...serious bike."

The Harley was the size of a horse. Black. Lots of chrome. And the pipes out the back were thicker than her upper arm. No wonder the thing sounded like an airplane.

"My one luxury." Spike jogged down the white marble steps. "Her name's Bette. As in Bette Davis."

Mad followed. "She looks more like a *he*. Named Butch."

Spike laughed. "Oh, no. Bette's a female. She's my girl. And I told her about you, so she'll be cool."

"You talk to your bike?"

"Of course. Now put this on."

He handed her the helmet then kicked his leg over the Harley's seat. He fit the machine perfectly. And those *pants*...

"Don't worry," he said as she hesitated, "I don't showboat on this thing. And when I have passengers, I always take it extra careful."

Just how many women had ridden with him? she wondered.

Spike flicked a key, rose up from the seat, and slammed his body downward. The bike lit off with a roar that she felt into her bones. Or maybe the buzz was more from the sight of his thighs straddling all that horsepower.

A *lot* of women, she decided, had been on that Harley with him. Because no one of the female persuasion would turn down an invitation like this.

"I think I love you," she blurted, overcome by the sight of him. Then slapped her hand over her mouth.

"What?" he said over the noise.

Oh, yeah...sure she was repeating that, even though she'd been joking. "Nothing."

She put the helmet on, fitted the strap under her chin and mounted the Harley. There wasn't a whole lot of room and her body immediately went flush with Spike's backside. With the bike vibrating and her legs cradling his hips, it was really hard not to think about very dangerous, very dumb things. Like what if they were facing each other. And—

"You ready?"

Oh, yes…she was.

Mad winced and then yelled over the noise, "What about your helmet?"

He looked over his shoulder, yellow eyes gleaming. "You're wearing it. Just hold on to me, okay?"

She put her hands on his tight waist, right above his leathers. Oh…boy. His body was hard all over. Warm, too.

"Where are we going?" she shouted.

"Anywhere. Nowhere. Away. That all right?"

"Yes…yes, it is."

He cranked one of the grips on the handlebars, the engine let out a growl and they were off. The bike was a living thing beneath them, the throbbing and the noise and the power humming through her body. With the warm air coming at her, and the moonlit road out in front, she felt like she must be dreaming.

Because real life just didn't come in this many shades of perfect.

Spike handled the Harley beautifully, shifting gears with smooth coordination, never going too fast or stopping too quickly. Before she knew it, she had relaxed against him and ended up with her hands all the way around his waist and her torso curved around his back. As she smelled fresh oil and his spicy aftershave and the lush summer night, she would have been quite content to keep going forever.

Eventually he pulled over on a secluded stretch of road and turned the bike off. Letting go of him was a tough one, but she did it quickly so he wouldn't think she was clinging. Kicking her leg up and out, she dismounted and took off the helmet, shaking loose her hair.

In the woods on either side of the road, crickets chimed and fireflies danced among the trees. Now that they weren't moving, the air was as soft as a sigh.

Spike snapped out the kickstand, but stayed on the bike, plugging his hands into his thighs, eyeing her steadily. "Sean told me how to find you, and as I said, I should have called. If you want me to go, I understand, but I wanted to at least show up and prove I was willing to make the drive even if you turned me away."

She craned her neck back and looked up at the stars. Then she focused on him. "I'd like you to stay."

"Good." His lips tilted up on one side. "So that means I'm your boy for this weekend. I'll do anything for you. You need me to freak your half brother out? Scare that butler again? Wash the dog? You just let me know."

How about kissing me, she thought, eyeing the thrust of his jaw and his jet-black hair and those wide shoulders.

Except that was ridiculous. He'd only showed up because he felt guilty. And because Sean had undoubtedly bullied him into it. He certainly hadn't come because he was interested in her. Spike had never shown one indication that he was attracted to her. The two of them were friends.

Yup. Story of her life. Friends.

But at least he came.

"We don't have a dog," she said.

"Cat?"

"Richard doesn't like animals."

"Figures."

"You know, you don't have to do this just because you feel badly about what you said." Shoot, why was she giving him an out?

"That's not the only reason why I'm here."

Her breath got tight. "Oh?"

An evil little light showed up in his yellow eyes and he smiled more broadly. "I'm dying to get to know your half brother better."

She laughed, thinking she probably shouldn't like it that he seemed to want to stand up for her. "I'm glad you came. I appreciate it."

"Then put 'er there." He offered her his hand. "We're a team this weekend, you and me."

She leaned forward and grasped his palm carefully. The contact was electric, a hot sizzle bolting up her arm and nailing her in the chest. And yet as she struggled to keep calm, he didn't linger or show any kind of reaction at all. He just gave her a solid shake and let go.

"So, partner," he said. "What else do you have on deck tonight? Anything?"

"Well, I usually swim after dinner."

"I brought my trunks."

"Then let's go back."

"Ah, yes, and the terrace is going to want to see us. So we shouldn't keep it up worrying about our safe return."

She laughed and then thought of Richard's party logistics. "Actually, maybe we should drive around a little longer. That way we can miss the whole après dinner thing."

"Hot damn." Spike clapped his hands together. "See, this is what I'm talking about. You and I are going to make a great pair. We already think alike."

He fired up the bike and looked at her with expectation.

Staring back at him hurt. He was so relaxed and easy. Because obviously being around her was uncomplicated.

Friends. Just…friends.

She mounted the Harley and put the helmet on, but Spike didn't set them in motion until he was sure she had the chin strap clipped together. She waited until they were going at quite a clip before sneaking her hands across his stomach and linking them together. It was pathetic, but the only reason she didn't lay her cheek on his shoulder was the bulky helmet.

Well, that and the fact they were…friends.

Chapter Five

By the time they got back to the house, the cars in front had all left and most of the lights were off. Mad hated letting go of Spike, but as he flipped out the kickstand and cut the Harley's engine, she lost the socially acceptable excuse to drape herself over him like a tarp.

"Place cleared out quick," he said as they dismounted.

"Richard likes to get up early." She removed the helmet and let it dangle from her hand. Then she looked the bike over. "Did you say you had things to bring in?"

"Yup." Spike nodded to the black leather saddlebags on either side of the Harley. "All I need is in there."

He leaned down and reached inside one of them, taking out a folded up duffel and snapping the thing open. With quick movements, he transferred over a bunch of rolled-up clothes and a dopp kit and she tried not to notice that there was nothing even vaguely pajama-like as far as she could see.

Then again she already knew from their night at Sean's that he preferred sleeping in the nude.

"You pack economically," she murmured.

"Coming from a sailor, that's a compliment, right?"

"Absolutely."

They went inside and were met by Richard's butler who insisted on taking Spike upstairs to his guest room. Mad went with them, following the two men all the way around to the opposite side of the house from her room.

If she and Spike had been any farther apart, he'd have been sleeping in the house next door.

She waited until the butler left.

"Will this be okay for you?" she asked, glancing around the formal room with its antiques and its hand-painted wallpaper.

Spike rolled his eyes and tested the plush bed with his heads. "Oh, I'll make do."

"The pool's out back," she said, going over to a window. "You can see it from here."

He came over and pushed the heavy satin drape out of the way. As he peered out around her, she shifted to the side and glanced back. She was very tall for a woman and physically strong as well, so it took a lot of man to make her feel dainty, feminine. Spike had four inches and at least seventy-five pounds on her, maybe more given the size of his shoulders. So he did the trick. Nicely.

God, they were so close that she could see the shadow of his beard growth and each and every one of his eyelashes. Her eyes locked on his lips.

"You want to meet down there?" he said. When she didn't answer, he frowned and looked at her. "Mad?"

"Ah—yes. That would be great." She stepped away. "Do you know how to find—"

"Don't worry about me." He smiled at her easily. "I'll get there."

She left and didn't remember walking to the other side of the house.

When she opened the door to her bedroom, however, she came back to reality with a jerk.

Everything inside had been done over. Everything was different.

No, not just different. Her imprint on this space had been eradicated.

The walls had once been a deep red she'd loved, a rich, powerful claret she'd chosen with her mother long ago. Now the room was a pastel rose, as if the color she'd liked had been exposed to too much sun and had faded. And then there was the lace. On the windows. On the bed. In the bath.

It was the kind of room Amelia would have liked.

Mad shook her head, wishing she'd been put somewhere else. Better that than to sleep in a place she'd once thought of as a sanctuary, but was now a kind of pink prison.

This was so alienating, she thought as she shut the door. She wasn't soft or muted or pretty and she didn't feel comfortable amid all the soft and muted and pretty in the room. Frankly, she found all the femininity…intimidating. Something she felt like she should have and appreciate, but just didn't.

Except then she thought of the bunks she'd crashed on for the last six weeks and all the things she'd done with the boys on the crew. When you were on a boat in the middle of the ocean, soft and muted and pretty got you classified as ballast. There, out on the sea, power was all that mattered and you needed it both in your head and your body. It was only on land that strength like that sometimes made women less than appealing.

Whatever. This was Richard's house and Richard's walls and Richard's windows and Richard's floor. She had no claim to any of it and she needed to let go of the past.

She changed into her bathing suit and was wrapping a towel around herself when a knock rang out. She opened the door and wished she hadn't.

"Oh…hello, Richard."

Her half brother had downshifted from the suit he'd worn at dinner into a cashmere V-neck and some slacks. He had a bored expression on his face, but those eyes of his were sharp as always. Clearly, he was on a mission.

He walked right in, forcing her to step back. "Swimming?" he said. "This late?"

"Part of my training schedule."

"As if you need more muscle." He looked around, cataloging her small bag and the pants and shirt she'd folded neatly and put on the dresser. "Where are the rest of your things?"

"Look, Richard, I was just going down to the pool—"

"To meet Spike, of course." Richard went over to one of the banks of lace drapery and shook a section of the stuff out. When he was satisfied with how the piece hung, he turned around. "So how did you meet that man? The two of you never did answer my question."

"It was through a friend."

"Who?"

"Sean."

"And how does Sean know him?"

Mad crossed her arms over her chest and took the fact

that she was getting pissed off as a good sign. It was better than cowering. "I have no clue."

"When did you first meet him? How long have you known him?"

"That doesn't matter."

"Then why not tell me?"

This was the problem with Richard, she thought. His mouth was fast and his reasoning was hard to get around. If she didn't answer him, she would seem petty.

"It was fairly recently," she hedged. "And we're just friends, Richard. You heard me at dinner."

"You don't look at him like he's a friend. So obviously he's the one who's not interested."

"Did you come here to make me feel bad? Or was there another purpose?"

He smiled at her a little. "Have I upset you?"

"Oh, not at all. The suggestion that a man couldn't possibly be attracted to me is a terrific thing to hear. Especially in your tone of voice."

"I'm sorry," he said smoothly. He glanced at her duffel bag. "I can't believe that's all you've brought for a whole weekend. Penelope would need a bag that size to go out to lunch properly."

And he made this sound as if the defect was Mad's, not the other woman's.

"Richard—"

"So." He clasped his hands together and pointed both forefingers straight at her chest. "I want you to play golf with me tomorrow. I'm inviting two friends of mine to the club and we're going out at one o'clock. But let's be clear. I do not want you to win by too much. Just a stroke or three, nothing more. The object is not to embarrass them like you've done with some of my other associates. You need to remember that no one likes losing to a woman on the links." He headed for the open door. "Oh, and by the way, one of them is just divorced. Maybe he'd be interested in you. His ex-wife was a model and I think he's had it with that beautiful, sociable type."

Mad closed her eyes. A command performance with a win spread coupled with a single guy who was a buddy of her half brother's. Just the way she'd hoped to spend a Saturday afternoon. "Richard."

He paused and looked over his shoulder. "Yes?"

"I'm sorry, I can't."

"Can't go? Why? Spending time with your chef?"

"As a matter of fact we have plans." Or they would as soon as they thought them up.

"So break them."

She met Richard's eyes steadily. Crucible...crucible... This was her crucible... "No."

Impatience flickered across his face and then his eyes narrowed. "Why did you come out here if you didn't want to spend time with your family?"

Because I'm going to boot you out of my trust for good, half brother. That's the only reason I made the trip.

"There's plenty of time left," she murmured. "But I will not go to the club with you tomorrow."

Richard measured her for a long time, as if trying to break her with all the silence. Then he shrugged.

"Fine. I'll get the pro to play. You always were a hermit, you know that?" He stepped out into the hall, then wrapped a hand around the jamb molding and leaned back in. "One more question about Spike. What is his last name?"

Oh, God. She couldn't answer that, could she? She only knew him as Spike....

Mad kept her tone mild even though she was about to lose it. "If you're so interested in him, ask him yourself."

Richard's eyes passed over her slowly. "You're not usually this difficult."

Welcome to the new world, she thought. And wait'll you see what else I've got planned for you.

"Maybe I'm just getting older."

"Somehow, I doubt that. Sleep well, Madeline." Richard didn't bother shutting the door behind him.

Mad wheeled away, burning with frustration—and found herself staring at the lace drapes he'd fiddled with so carefully. Though it made her immature as hell, she walked across the room, shoved her hands into the delicate fall, and shook them into a mess.

It didn't make her feel any better. Instead, she was just ashamed of herself for being so petty.

She left the room and headed down to the pool, working herself up into a lather. Her half brother had been taking potshots at her since she'd been in diapers, and as a child she'd accepted the taunting cruelty as the way of the world, something like bad thunderstorms and monsters in the closet and any meal that had tuna fish in it.

But she wasn't a five-year-old to be clipped into place. Not anymore.

As she stepped out of the house, a rhythmic splashing sound got her attention.

The estate's Olympic-size pool was set into the ground on the far side of a slate terrace. Lights glowed around its periphery, the soft illumination picking out the square, boxwood hedging and the Brown Jordan patio furniture. But none of that was important.

The male body churning through the water was doing the freestyle, long arms and powerful shoulders eating up the distance, the rhythmic surging of the strokes…potent, sexual.

Mad walked over, dropped her towel on a chaise and watched Spike swim. When he got to the far side, he executed a perfect kick-turn and shot out from the wall, his stroke resuming easily.

Focusing on him was a lot more enjoyable than thinking of Richard, she decided. But not really more relaxing.

As Spike kicked out from the wall and resurfaced, he figured he'd done about a half mile already. But he still had plenty of energy to burn off.

That ride with Mad had been an exercise in torture. Her hands around his waist, her torso curved against his spine, her body close as their clothes would allow. He could have cheerfully taken them to South Dakota and back and still not have wanted to get off the bike.

That woman was like nothing he'd ever been near before. Capable of lighting him up like a football stadium just because she came into a room. And man, did he have to fight not to let the reaction show.

Spike got to the shallow end of the pool and stopped. Planting his feet on the bottom, he pushed his torso out of the water, flipped his hair back and breathed hard.

"Hi."

He pivoted to the left. Mad was standing on the terrace in a sports bikini, nothing but skin and curves and strength.

And wouldn't you know it, his body responded. In a rush.

Thank God the underwater lights weren't on.

"Hi." He lifted his arm up in greeting.

She sat down on the pool's edge, dangling her long, beautiful legs in the warm, splashing depths. "You're a good swimmer."

"I like the water." More now that there was some of her in it.

"Me, too." She watched her feet as she moved them up and down.

"Something wrong? You look tense."

"Oh, it's nothing." She glanced up and smiled. "Well, nothing a good workout won't cure."

In the blink of an eye, she was up and diving into the pool, a clean slice of female flesh cutting through the water.

Not surprisingly, she was a fantastic swimmer. She set off at a bruising pace, churning through the water, her body perfectly synchronized. He resumed his own strokes, matching his rhythm to hers until they were doing the laps together. She didn't let up on the speed and they went hard for a good half hour, doing a mile or maybe two. Eventually, he had to bite at the water with his arms to keep up with her and then she pulled ahead: the weights he lifted all the time were good for building muscle, but she maxed him out cardiovascularly.

Finally, she stopped at the deep end, and hung on to the edge of the pool. Half a minute later, he pulled in next to her and tried to catch his breath.

"That was a good haul," she said, smiling.

As she draped both her arms up on the smooth concrete lip, she leisurely kicked her legs to cool down.

Meanwhile, he did his best not to notice all the droplets of water that clung to her skin. Or the way her nipples had tightened against the chill.

"I like swimming with a buddy," she said.

Spike shoved his hair out of his face. A buddy. That's right. Buddy, as in friend. As in no looking. And no kissing or touching…no licking…

"So do I." But he couldn't manage to smile back at her.

Oh man…all he could think about was reaching through the water for her. Dragging her against his body. Sliding his thigh between her legs. Pushing his hips forward until—

Mad playfully nudged his shoulder with her foot. "Now you're the one looking all tense. Usually workouts bring people down."

"Sorry." —their lower bodies fused. Then he would wrap his arms all the way around her and—

"Hey, would you like to watch a movie?"

"Ah…yeah."—kiss her deep and hard until she—

"We have a screening room. And no one else will be up. I'm the insomniac in the family. Well, Richard, too, but he doesn't really like movies, either…"

Stop it, Moriarty, he told himself. Just stop the fantasizing routine or you're never going to get out of this water.

"So is it a plan?" she asked.

"Yeah."

Mad pushed off the side of the pool and went over to the ladder. Her shoulders flexed as she pulled herself out, the water sluicing down her body. As she turned to face him again, she gathered her hair up and squeezed the wetness out of it.

Crystal tears clung to her skin, sparkling in the low light.

Her smile was off-the-charts lovely. "You, Spike, look like an action-flick kind of guy. How about a *Die Hard* marathon?"

Spike just blinked. Clearly, she'd switched over to a

foreign language because he was no longer tracking a word she was saying.

She swung her hair onto her back and bent over for her towel. "My favorite character in the first one was Argyle." As she wrapped up, she frowned. "Spike? You feeling okay?"

Oh, he was feeling just fine. Uh-huh.

For a guy whose head was about to explode.

And damn it, she wasn't even aware of him, was she? She had no idea what she was doing to him as she moved in the warm night air.

"Spike?"

"Tell you what, you go on ahead. I'm going to finish up here."

"Oh, come on. You've got to be tired. You started before I came."

"Later, Mad. I'll be up later."

She dropped her eyes. As she fell silent, the hum of the pool filter seemed to get louder. "Ah, hell…I did it again, didn't I."

"Did what?" he asked.

"Look, I'm sorry. And we can forget about the movie." She shook her head. Looked back at the house. "I guess I'll…I'll just see you in the morning."

"Mad, what the hell are you sorry for?"

"Nothing. I'll see—"

"What's wrong?"

"I just didn't think." She put her hands on her hips. Frowned. "You know, about the whole…swimming thing."

"Excuse me?"

"It's nothing." She cocked her leg up and rubbed her ankle a little, as if on reflex. Her eyes refused to meet his.

"Oh, before I forget. Breakfast is at eight sharp. If you're not there, you won't get to eat until lunch. 'Night."

As she turned away, he said sharply, "What's going on here, Mad?"

When she stopped and faced him again, he was relieved—given that he couldn't go after her, not with the erection he was sporting.

With a quick move, she repositioned the towel, tightening it over her breasts. His eyes latched on to the subtle curves.

Stop it.

"Partners talk to each other, Mad. What's wrong?"

"Oh, it's… Yeah, nothing new. Most men don't like the way I swim. Or play golf. Or lift weights. Or run." She shrugged. "They don't like it when I can out-drive them on the fairway or go faster around the track or go harder in the water."

Spike could only stare at her. "Where the hell did you get that idea?"

She rolled her eyes. "Richard reminded me again tonight. Just ask him, he'll explain the whole—"

"No offense, but I wouldn't ask your half brother what day of the week he thought it was. And I can't believe you think so little of me."

Her eyes shifted to his. "Well, you're clearly tense so I assume you're upset about something."

"And you think it's because you can out-lap me?"

She shrugged. "It's happened before."

"Not with me. I love the fact that you can swim hard."

Her eyes narrowed. After a moment, the tight lines of her face relaxed.

"Really?" she said, a little smile lighting on her lips. "Because that would be great. That would be…really great."

"And I want to watch Bruce Willis with you. Or Bambi. Or…whatever." Hell, he never wanted the night to end.

Now she beamed. "So let's go."

There was another stretch of silence as he tried to figure out what to do considering the condition he was in.

She tilted her head to the side. "You don't want to get out of the pool, do you. Why?"

Well…they were both adults here, weren't they? And it wasn't as if she'd never seen an aroused man before. Besides, she was bound to figure out how he felt sometime during the course of the weekend and it seemed more honest to get it out of the way on the first night.

Spike swam over to the ladder she'd used and slowly dragged his body out of the water. He knew exactly when she saw what was doing. Her eyes peeled open and she took a stumbling step backward.

Guess they were clear on that.

He quickly covered himself with a towel. "Tell you what. Why don't we take a rain check on the movie, okay?"

She just stood there staring at him, clearly not inclined to say much. Which made him feel even more like a total letch.

"Good night, Mad."

He walked into the house and headed for the second floor. As he went, his internal cursing jammed up his head so badly it was a wonder he could find his room at all.

Except then he had something else to think about. As soon as he opened the door, his instincts went off, warning bells replacing the regret recital. Something was not right.

He closed himself in and looked around. Over on the bureau, his wallet was in a subtly different position than he'd left it in. And at the foot of the bed, the strap of his duffel was off to one side, no longer laying in the middle of the bag.

Now he cursed out loud. When you'd been in prison, you knew all about having your things searched both on purpose and in secret, both by folks who knew what they were doing and others who didn't. This had been an amateur job. Someone had been sufficiently careful that to the casual eye, you wouldn't think anything had been disturbed. But Spike knew what had been done.

He checked through his stuff and wasn't surprised that nothing had been taken. It was a classic, sloppy sneak and peek.

Not what he'd expected. Not what he wanted.

His full name was the door to his past. And he'd just as soon make it through the weekend without Mad knowing a damn thing. She had enough on her hands with that half brother of hers; no reason for her to worry that she'd invited an ex-con home.

Spike took a quick shower and got into bed, feeling distinctly exposed. As he leaned back against the headboard, all he could think about was what had happened after he'd told that other woman he'd dated about the death he'd caused.

For some reason, he couldn't bear the idea that Mad would have the same response, that she would see him only as some kind of murderer. He could live with being socially and financially beneath her. What he couldn't handle was her being frightened of him.

He'd just turned the light off when there was a knock.

"Yeah?" he said, sitting up.

The door opened a crack.

"Can I come in for a sec?" Mad's voice was low.

He yanked the covers up to his chest, very aware of how naked he was. "Ah…sure."

When she closed the door behind her, he turned the light

back on. She was in a black satin bathrobe, her hair dry as if she'd washed it and blown it out. She smelled of the fancy French soap he'd used on himself, as if the whole house was stocked with the stuff. The scent was perfect for her.

As Mad paced around, it seemed like she was working up the nerve to say something, and while silence stretched out, all he could do was watch. And want.

She halted at the foot of the bed. "Are you honestly attracted to me?"

Totally. Completely.

"Ah…yeah. I am." His eyes lingered on her pale neck and the V where the two halves of the robe came together. "But don't worry, I'm not an animal or anything. I know how to keep my hands to myself."

"Why?"

"Sorry, what?"

"Why are you attracted to me?"

Spike frowned. The woman didn't want him, but was all set to hear the eight thousand things he liked about her? Like she needed the ego boost?

That she was so shallow was a surprise.

"Whatever, Mad. Go back to your room, okay? I'll see you in the morning."

She seemed to pale, but then she nodded and took off. Almost as if she were ashamed.

Man, what the hell was that all about?

Spike turned off the light and eased back against the pillows. A split second later, he threw the covers off himself and dragged on a pair of nylon sweats.

Mad rushed down the hall, feeling like an idiot. Whatever attraction Spike had had toward her down at the pool hadn't lasted long. He'd seemed disgusted with her just now.

Yeah, well, maybe it was because she was so damn naive. Someone like him, who'd no doubt had…oh, God, *dozens* of lovers, wouldn't be interested in a repressed, sexually insecure woman like her.

And though she wished things were different, she couldn't pretend confidence in the sexual arena. After having been compared unfavorably to the female standard for decades by her father and half brother, after having had men she really liked forget she even existed after they met Amelia, after having lived on boats with guys for four years just like she was one of them, the idea a man wanted her was just… a total flipping surprise.

Then there was the fact that it was Spike.

But she couldn't have handled the situation down at the pool worse, could she? When he'd gotten out of the water, she hadn't been prepared for the arousal she'd seen. It had been so unexpected she'd taken a step back out of shock. Which was, of course, not the best reaction if you were actually interested in the guy.

"Mad, wait up!" came from behind her.

She looked over her shoulder. Spike was naked to the waist and coming after her at a jog.

As she got to her bedroom, she rushed to open the door and then slipped inside, not wanting to deal. Except before she could shut him out, Spike crammed his body in the way.

His eyes bored into hers in the tense silence. She wanted to move. Couldn't make herself turn away.

He looked over her hair, her throat, lower. "I didn't come to Greenwich to get in bed with you."

Like she needed to hear that? "Of course you didn't—"

"But I can't keep myself from wanting you."

Mad's lungs stopped working. Holy…did he just say that?

Yes, you idiot, she thought.

"Do you still want to know why I'm attracted to you?" he whispered.

Feeling like she were sky diving, she said, "Yes."

"Then let me in."

Slowly, she opened the door wide. He was the one who shut it.

He stared at her for the longest time. And then he said, quiet as a breath, "How could I not want you? You're beautiful."

He reached out and took some of her hair into his wide palm, bringing it to his nose. Then he dropped the dark waves and touched the side of her face, his thumb brushing over her temple.

She jumped as his other hand went to her shoulder.

"Easy," he murmured. "I'm not going to hurt you."

As he held her face, he caressed her body, that light touch moving up and down her arms, her waist, her hip, across her back…and then around to the front. He was telling her what he liked without words and it was…everything about her.

His hand stopped over her heart and his head bent down to her ear.

"Mad?" His voice was a deep rumble.

She couldn't breathe. She absolutely couldn't breathe. "Yes?"

"Will you let me kiss you?"

"Yes," she sighed.

"Good." He pulled back and cupped her face. "Because every time I see your mouth, that's all I can think of doing."

He covered her lips smoothly, slanting his head, pressing in, arms sliding around her. His mouth moved in a slow, patient way, easing her, enticing her. He was a master at this, she realized. A master at the holding and the taking, his big hard body exactly the kind of anchor she needed to keep standing.

He ended the kiss by shifting away just a little. His cheeks were flushed, his skin heated, his lower body... aroused. She could feel his need against her and was dizzy from the promise of that hard rope of his.

"Don't stop," she said, slipping her arms around his neck and bringing him back down.

They kissed forever, bodies melding, mouths moving, hands touching. At some indefinable point, the tenor of it all changed from exploration to a restless, growing hunger.

"Mad..." Spike broke off the kiss and buried his face in her neck. Without warning, his teeth bit down on her a little, then he licked where he'd nipped her. His breath was hot on her skin, his big body straining with need.

But he was reining himself in for her. In this pause, he was controlling himself.

"Mad, just how far do you want this to go?"

She eyed the bed from over his shoulder, wanting to be in it with him. And yet fearing that, too. He was a man to get lost in and even professional sailors couldn't always save themselves from drowning.

"I don't know."

"Then I need to stop now."

He stepped back and shook his head as if trying to clear it. Then he turned, did something to the front of his sweatpants, and faced her again with a rueful smile.

"Actually, Mad, it's better we don't...go there. Honestly, I didn't come here for that, in spite of what just happened. All I want to do is help you through the weekend."

Mad dragged in a deep breath and told herself he was

right. What was she doing, thinking of having sex with a man she barely knew? For the very first time in her life?

And yet somehow the he's-just-a-stranger rationale didn't hold water. She felt like she knew him right through his skin, down to his heart.

Spike kissed his forefinger and placed it on her lips. "Don't worry, Mad. We're going to get you to Monday without any more complications than absolutely necessary."

After he left and the door shut, Mad walked around, feeling like the bedroom was a very well-decorated hamster cage. Eventually, she stopped in front of a window.

The air-conditioning was on in the house, but she desperately needed some fresh air. Flipping the sash's lock, she threw her shoulder into the effort of getting the thing open, and finally it popped and squeaked. Real air poured into the room, smelling like the night-blooming roses in the garden below.

Getting down on her knees, she propped her forearms on the sill, put her chin on her wrists, and wished he had stayed.

She was twenty-five years old, for God's sake. Twenty-five, not fifteen. Which meant if she found a man she wanted as a lover, she could have him if he wanted her. And Spike had very definitely wanted her.

So why shouldn't they be together?

Mad blew out her breath.

Well, for one thing, he'd said he hadn't come for any kind of quick affair—good Lord, was he with someone already?

No, she thought. Sean would know that and Sean would have told her. Besides, Spike hadn't seemed as if he were dating anyone when the Doublemint Twins had been on his lap at that party.

So if he didn't have a woman in his life, why—

Oh, what was she thinking. Even if he were free as a jaybird, she didn't imagine he'd be in any hurry to get horizontal if he knew she was a virgin. Virginity in a woman, like physical strength, tended to make men a little jumpy. And not in a good way. Hell, maybe Spike would think she'd stalk him like some lovelorn teenager when he left at the end of the weekend.

Shoot, she probably would be tempted to do that already. There was something about that man that made her want to be as close to him as the very clothes he wore. It was those dangerous, dark looks of his. And the fact that over dinner he'd seemed ready to take Richard out back when the man had insulted her. And it was the way Spike had handled that Harley.

But mostly it was the look in his eyes when they met hers. There was kindness in him, deep reserves of kindness.

And that kindness meant she could trust him.

Chapter Six

Thank God for this pool, Spike thought the next morning.

As he stroked through the water, he was working off the burn from an entire night of erotic dreams. Some had been conscious, playing on the ceiling above him as he stared up sightlessly, his hips throbbing with the need to release. But the worst of them had come after he'd slid into an agitated sleep. In those, he could actually feel the heat of her body against his own.

Man, this whole thing with Madeline Maguire was trouble.

Sure, he'd always liked women, had had some pretty heavy-duty sexual needs. Except nothing came close to what he felt like with Mad. During that one kiss with her, he'd become all instinct, nothing but rank male starvation. Holding her, pushing his body against hers, straining like he was lifting a car off the ground, he'd felt as if he'd never had a woman before and would never have one again.

So this was not good. Desperation was no one's friend in this world and that's what he'd been. Desperate. Half insane. Needy and out of control.

And the effect had lingered. Was still with him.

When he was finished with his last lap, he shot out of the pool and dried off, feeling the coming warmth of the day already. Linking the towel around his neck, he stared past the pool at a spread right out of *House & Garden*. The acreage behind the mansion was landscaped to within an inch of its life: carefully selected bushes were clipped into precise shapes, fancy blooming flowers were corralled into beds, lawn was clipped tight as a beard, as if someone had taken a buzz razor to it instead of a mower.

He thought of Mad growing up in this environment. She was too vibrant for all this control. No wonder she preferred the sea....

Well, and then there was her half brother who'd drive anyone off the side of a continent.

Funny, Spike thought. When he'd decided to come to help her out, it hadn't really mattered why she and her half brother didn't get along. Now, he wanted to know the *why* of everything about her.

"You better hurry or you'll miss breakfast."

He turned at the sound of her voice. She was standing on the terrace wearing faded jeans and a navy blue polo shirt. Her dark hair was shining in the morning sun and she looked even better than she had in all those dreams he'd had last night.

His heart tripped over itself and fell into his gut. "Hey."

She focused on the gardens beyond him. "Enjoying the view?"

Now he was. "Quite an estate you have."

"Oh, it's never been mine. First it was my father's. Now it's Richard's."

Spike walked around the deep end of the pool so they weren't talking over all the water. And the closer he got to her, the more he remembered what she felt like against him.

She smiled at the towel around his neck. "I'm serious about changing fast. If you want food, you better get a move on."

"How about going out for breakfast with me?" He really didn't want to sit at a table with her and her half brother and get served by the butler. He wanted her relaxed. At ease. Talking. "There's got to be somewhere around here that serves pancakes."

Her smile was slow. "I think I can find you something you'll like."

They were on the Harley fifteen minutes later and heading into town. Because it was early, they had the streets mostly to themselves and for Spike, the day seemed to overflow with possibilities.

But then having the woman you wanted on the back of your bike would do that to a guy.

The place she took them to was barely big enough to house the long line of Saturday morning sweet roll shoppers at its counter. The little café had only six tables the size of chessboards off to one side and not even room for a coat rack. Cinnamon permeated the air and so did the down-home smell of baking dough.

"Everyone gets their scones and muffins here," Mad said as they wended in and out of the dozen or so folks standing in front of an Order Here sign. "But they also do great Belgian waffles, which is close to pancakes, right?"

"Absolutely. I was just after the maple syrup, anyway."

As they sat down, Spike tried to keep his grin to himself. The great advantage of having two tall people at one little table was that knees touched. Feet brushed. Ankles found ankles.

"Sorry," she said, retracting her legs.

"Don't pull back on my account," he all but growled.

Her eyes shot to his and they both froze. In less than a nanosecond, all he could think about was throwing her over his shoulder and taking her somewhere very private. He even eyed the door.

Whoa…men really were awful, weren't they?

"Hi, can I get you some coffee?"

As the waitress slid long sheets of mint-green paper onto the table, Spike closed his eyelids and cracked his neck.

Damn it, he was tight as a steel cable. All over.

"That'd be great," he said to the woman. Although the last thing he needed was more stimulation.

The menus were printed with the words *Summer Breakfast Selections* at the top and they listed all manner of carbohydrates.

Spike just stared a hole in his without tracking much of anything. He was too aware of every move Mad made across from him: the way she pushed her hair over her shoulder, played with the collar of her polo, shifted in the chair and recrossed her legs.

When the coffee landed, the two giant cups made him wonder where the food would fit on the table. Mad took hers up with relish, sighing as she sipped and he ordered the waffles.

"What about you?" he asked.

She lowered the fat, crockery mug. "This is perfect. Well, maybe two of these."

He frowned, then just figured she wasn't a breakfast person.

"Mind if I ask you something personal?" he said after the waitress had left.

Mad rested her coffee on her knee and smiled at him. "Not at all."

"Did you grow up with Richard? I mean, was he in the house a lot?" Because Spike couldn't imagine the guy had been any easier to deal with back in the good old days. Richard had no doubt only been a smaller, higher-pitched version of what he'd become as an adult.

"Yes, I grew up with him. His mother and my father divorced when Richard was six. Back then, kids usually stayed with their moms, but there was no way Richard Maguire, Sr. would have that. Much later, I heard that Father paid the woman a lot to get her to relinquish her parental rights."

"She just walked away?"

"As far as I know, neither Richard nor Amelia has seen her since."

"That's cold—wait, you have a half sister, too?"

Mad picked up her mug and held it in front of her mouth. "Yes."

"What about your mom?"

"She was Father's second wife and she was taken away from us too soon. I was four." Mad took a long sip, a little whistling noise coming out from between her lips as she drank. Then she said, "But at least I have some memories of her."

"I'm very sorry."

"Thanks, but it was long ago."

"What was your father like?"

The coffee went right up in front of her mouth again, obviously a clue she was feeling awkward. "He was... my father."

"We can change the subject."

"No...it's okay. My father...ah, he was a lot like Richard. The two of them look alike."

"And did they act alike, as well?"

She lowered the mug and traced a pattern on the tabletop with her finger. "Let's just say prep school was a relief. Matter of fact, I begged to go. And it wasn't just that Richard and my father could be very cutting. I was always out of place at home."

"How so?"

"Richard and Amelia are like Barbie dolls. Fair, blond. Perfect. Especially Amelia. Amelia is truly beautiful. She's spectacular."

"Spectacular depends on who's doing the looking." For example, he was staring at spectacular right now.

"Oh, but you haven't seen her. Men go nuts over her. Me? I was this lonely, lanky tomboy who wanted to be in the Olympics." She frowned. "You know, it's strange. I like myself. I like who I am. I love what I'm doing. But every time I come home, I just hear my father's voice in my head. Or Richard's in my ear."

"Straight up, your half brother's a pain in the ass."

"I know." She smiled. "He's always been difficult. Though I have to say, our father was equally hard on him. Richard excelled at school and then in business, but it was never good enough. None of us were good enough for Father. I was the sports without the grace. Amelia was the beauty without the depth. Richard was the brains without the brawn. Father used to say, if the three of us were one person, we could really be something. I coped by leaving. Richard coped by turning into him."

"And Amelia?"

Mad's face became a mask. "She had other ways of getting positive male attention… But listen, enough about my family. Let's talk about you."

Let's not, he thought.

"You don't like to, do you?" she murmured.

"I'm sorry?"

"Talk about yourself."

Fortunately, the waitress showed up with his food. He had to lean away as a plate that took up most of the table was put down in front of him. To help make space, Mad palmed her mug and eased back in her chair.

"Can I get you to share this with me?" he asked while the waitress topped off Mad's cup.

"Oh, no. I'm fine."

He picked up the pitcher of maple syrup that had come with his eats. "You ate before?"

"I'm not big into breakfast. Although I have to say that looks fantastic." After the waitress left, Mad said, "Spike? You can trust me."

"I know."

"Do you?"

He nodded, not wanting to keep things from her, but unwilling to drag her down. "Yeah, I do."

He bit into the waffles and they were great, light and tasting of vanilla…although it wasn't as if he could truly savor them. Mad's soft words had landed in his gut and were taking up most of the space down there.

Trust… Sure he could trust her, but he'd come to help her, not freak her out.

He was halfway through the first waffle when she said, "There's something you should know."

"About?"

"Last night."

He fell still and looked up at her. "What…about last night?"

The blush that hit her cheeks was absolutely gorgeous. "I wanted you to stay."

Breath eased out of his lungs. "God…I wanted that, too."

"I'm just not… I'm not into casual sex."

"I didn't think you were." And he loved that about her.

"In fact—"

"Madeline? Is that you?"

Spike frowned at the low male voice. When he looked up, there was a dark-haired man looming over the table. The guy had sunglasses on, of an expensive variety, and he was sporting that casual, I'm-a-rich-guy-in-the-summer thing, all linen-shirted and khaki-shorted. His watch was gold, almost the size of the table and screamed ROLEX.

"Mick!" Mad said with delight. "What are you doing here?"

Good question, Spike thought.

Mad stood up, keeping her mug with her because there was no place to put it down. She was surprised to see her lawyer in Greenwich, but then the town wasn't that far from the city and it was a holiday weekend.

Mick smiled a little, his hard expression loosening some as he jogged a paper bag in his hand. "I've got a weakness for their corn muffins."

Funny, it was tough to imagine the man having a weakness for anything.

She glanced downward. "I'd ask you to join us—"

"Don't think I could fit at the table." Her attorney stuck his hand out toward Spike. "Mick Rhodes."

As Spike shook the palm that was offered, his yellow eyes were intent, as if he were measuring every molecule of the other man.

"Are you visiting Greenwich?" Mad asked.

"Live here."

"I didn't know you had a house in town."

"The old Murray place."

"Wow, that was a train wreck." Mad winced. Oh, way to be smooth. "I mean—"

"Not anymore it's not." Rhodes smiled coolly then dropped his voice. "Have you talked to Richard yet?"

"No, but soon. I just arrived last night."

"If you need me—" Rhodes reached into his pocket "—call me at home."

He wrote a number on the back of the business card and gave it to her. After she thanked him, she watched him walk through the customers.

"He's so amazing," she murmured as she sat back down in her chair again.

Spike made a low noise. Like a cough. "How so?"

"He's really good at what he does."

Spike stared across the café as the door shut behind her lawyer. "How do you know him?"

"Through Sean. The whole reason I came this weekend is because I've got some issues with my trust that I have to settle with Richard. I needed some good legal advice and Mick certainly gave it to me."

They were silent until Spike wiped his mouth and carefully laid his silverware down on his plate. He'd eaten all of the waffles in a neat and orderly way, his table manners superb.

When the waitress brought the check, he reached into his back pocket.

"I think Mad wants a refill," he said as he took out his wallet.

While her mug got refreshed, she watched him move in the little chair as his big body shifted. Those tattoos on each side of his neck undulated with his skin.

She wanted to kiss them.

He checked the bill, put a twenty on the handwritten slip, then covered the thing with a ten. "No change."

The waitress's eyes widened. "Thank you. Thank you very much."

"That was generous," Mad said with approval after the woman left.

"Do you have any idea how hard it is to wait on someone?" His eyes flashed up. "Probably not, though, right?"

His tone wasn't condemning or anything. Just factual.

It stung anyway.

"No, I've never waitressed." She frowned. "But I know how to scrub a boat deck until my hands bleed."

He grimaced. "I'm sorry, that could have come out better, couldn't it?"

She put her coffee down and stood up. "It's okay."

But it really wasn't. Something in the way he'd said the words lingered. When they were outside next to the bike, she said, "Would you think of me differently if I didn't come from money?"

"No. I'd still want to be your friend." He handed her the helmet.

Friend? But last night he'd wanted to…

Oh, come on, Maguire, she thought. Men could be sexually intimate with women they thought of as just friends. She'd seen it with her crew. Countless times.

But she needed to know something. "Spike, you're not with anyone right now, are you?"

He swung onto the bike and muscled it off its kickstand. "You mean a woman? No, I'm not."

His tone of voice was level, his facial expression bland. And that was when an essential truth about him slid into place. It was so obvious, she was amazed she hadn't noticed it before.

Spike had a secret.

For all his jovial, BMOC charisma at Sean's, Spike was one of those people who didn't cast a social shadow. There was no real footprint of information about him, except what the eye registered and what the here and now presented you with in terms of his character. The almost bored look he was putting out now was how he did it; he had a very smooth deflection system, giving the impression that there was nothing interesting or relevant about his past at all.

Of course, he had told her a few things back at Sean's... Except as she thought about what he'd said about his family, she decided he'd talked like that only because the details had held no great controversy for him. He hadn't seemed upset that he'd grown up without a father. And clearly his love for his sister and mother was likewise uncomplicated.

"When was the last serious relationship you had?" she asked, not caring that she was bumping into his barriers.

He frowned, turned the bike's key, and started to lift up, preparing to slam start the engine. "Ah, years. Years ago."

She stopped him by putting her hand on his forearm. "What happened?"

He shrugged. "We went our separate ways. I'm no good at relationships and no longer interested in them."

He started the bike. In the roaring noise, he seemed totally relaxed, until she looked at his eyes. They were fixated out on the road and narrowed to the point of being slits. He did not want to continue the conversation.

She wanted to ask why, but knew that would be rude as hell. Besides, she was already pushing her luck.

Mad put on the helmet and got up on the Harley behind him. As he gunned the bike, she latched on to his waist.

While they went back to the house, she began to wonder if she hadn't just read too much into him, though. Maybe he wasn't hiding something. Maybe he was only remembering what she seemed to forget: they'd only just met. People didn't always share intimate things with folks they didn't really know.

Yeah, maybe she was over-thinking.

And as for him not wanting a relationship, that wasn't a big surprise. It was obvious if he needed a woman, he could find one. He just had no use for a female in his life on a permanent basis.

For some reason, that hurt. Probably because what had happened between them the night before had been very special to her, but was no doubt just standard operating procedure for him.

God, she was such a romantic, wasn't she?

Mad shifted closer against him, linking her hands around his stomach, bringing her breasts flat against his back. As she thought about kissing him, feeling his body against hers, getting lost in his strength and his heat, the situation between them grew treacherously simple, dangerously clear.

She wasn't going to find that kind of passion anytime soon with someone else.

He was with her now.

And life was to be lived.

As temptation rose, it eclipsed even the thundering sound and the vibrations of the bike.

It was over lunch that Spike realized Mad didn't eat.

For the past half hour, they'd been sitting with Richard and Penelope in a sun-filled solarium. As talk had focused on the New York foodie scene, Mad had pushed her chicken salad around, cut up the lettuce leaves under it, fooled with the stuffed tomato on the side…and hadn't lifted her fork to her lips once.

As the butler cleared the dishes, she smiled at the man and shook her head when he asked if she wanted fruit for dessert. Then she tapped her iced tea glass for a refill.

Spike thought of all the coffee she'd had with breakfast. The woman was running on caffeine and not much else. And he might have been able to understand it if she was just uncomfortable around her half brother. But Richard hadn't been at the café this morning.

Penelope put her napkin down. "Will you excuse me? I'm going to go get ready to head to the club."

"I'll meet you in front in twenty minutes," Richard said.

"I'll be prompt." She smiled, patted his hand, and walked purposely out of the room.

Richard glanced over at Spike. "Will you give me a moment alone with my sister?"

Spike looked at Mad and cocked an eyebrow. When she shook her head slowly, he leaned back in his chair and got good and damned comfortable.

Richard's annoyance was obvious, but then he shrugged a little and produced a leather, legal-size folio from under his chair. He slid the thing across the glass table and put a black fountain pen on top of it.

"What is this?" Mad asked.

"I've done you a favor. It keeps the status quo with respect to your trust. I had my secretary flag where you need to sign in case you couldn't figure out what those lines at the end were for."

Oh, hell, no, Spike thought. No one took that kind of attitude with Mad, not while he was in the room.

He opened his mouth, but Mad put her hand on his arm and stopped him. "Richard, I have something I need to say."

"Then perhaps you should talk to a mirror." Richard got up, checked his watch and let his napkin fall into his seat. "I'm off to play golf now. Oh, and the guests arrive tonight at six. Please be on time. It should be easier for you as there won't be any traffic."

"Richard, I need you to listen—"

The man turned his back on her and headed out of the room, talking over his shoulder. "I want those signed now so they can be couriered to my lawyer in the city. Thank you for your cooperation."

Mad shot to her feet. "*Richard.*"

Her half brother stopped and pivoted on his loafers. His face was frozen, as if he'd never heard that tone of voice before and didn't like it.

Showdown time, Spike thought, glad he was in the room.

Richard's eyes narrowed. "I beg your pardon."

"I'm not signing these." Mad put her hand on top of the folio.

"Excuse me?"

"In fact, I'm filing to remove you as executor."

The change in the man was eerie. For a split second, his eyes flashed with fury, then no emotion showed in his face at all. "Why would you want to do that, Madeline?"

"It's time I took over my shares. Nothing more."

"Why now?"

"It's just…time."

"You don't know anything about business."

"I'll learn."

"How? On one of your boats?"

"Yes."

"You are aware, are you not, that Value Shop is a billion-dollar-a-year enterprise."

"Whether it's that or a mom and pop store, the shares are mine. I want to be responsible for them."

"You haven't earned the right to vote them. You don't know a P&L from a paper clip." He smiled, as if she were a five-year-old who was asking to eat crayons for dinner. "Why don't you stay out on the ocean where you belong and leave the business and the numbers to people who can handle them."

Spike couldn't keep his mouth shut a moment longer. "How about you dial down that tone of voice, buddy?"

"Perhaps you'll do me the *favor* of keeping out of this," Richard snapped.

Spike rose to his feet. "Like I said, lose the edge when you speak to her, my man."

"It's all right," Mad said, reaching out for his hand and tugging him back down into his chair. "No matter what he says, he can't change the outcome."

There was a long silence and then Richard's eyes settled

on Spike. "Oh, I get it. Well, at least I understand why you came with her."

Spike frowned, wondering just what kind of conclusion the guy had jumped to.

Mad pushed her hands into her pockets and tilted up her chin. "Richard, you can tell your lawyer not to hold his breath because you're getting no ink from me this afternoon. In fact, I'm going to go pack now. The only reason I came here was to get this conversation over with."

Richard's voice cooled out. "This isn't finished between us."

"The hell it's not."

There was another stretch of silence. Then Richard said, "I'll tell you what. The chairman of the board is coming tonight. Stay until then. Matter of fact, stay through Monday when I host the shareholder's picnic. All of the trustees will be there."

"Why?" Mad countered. "So you can try and set me up in front of them? You're not going to stop this."

"Then what do you have to lose, Madeline? If you've got me against the proverbial ropes, why not meet the chairman face-to-face tonight. Because you've never even seen him before, have you? You don't know him at all, do you? If you want to be a trustee in more than name only, then it makes sense to meet the man at the head of the table, doesn't it?"

Richard's expression was as smooth as pudding. And if Spike hadn't been a poker player, he might have bought the I-don't-care routine. Instead, he focused on the guy's flared nostrils and knew Mad's half brother wasn't quite as relaxed as he wanted to appear.

"Do you still vote Amelia's shares?" Mad asked.

"Yes, and she hasn't complained. Neither have you. Until now." Richard's eyes drifted to Spike. "Funny how things change." The man rechecked his watch. "I'll leave you two to decide what to do. Just permit me a social grace. If you decide to leave, have the courtesy of letting the butler know so he doesn't set places for you at the table. And remember, for every action, there is a complete and opposite reaction. You might consider the laws of physics before you try and take me on, sister."

Richard left and Mad eased down into her chair. With a heavy breath, she put her head in her hands.

Spike leaned over to her, laid his palm on her back, and rubbed her shoulder. Her body started jerking, little hiccupping sounds rising up from her tucked position.

"Mad, I'm sorry that was so tough."

Her face lifted and slowly turned to his.

She was smiling, laughing.

"I did it! I stood up to him." Mad giggled some more. "And we're going to damn well stay for dinner. I want to meet that chairman!"

Spike grinned back at her, but then lost the expression. He wanted to tell her he was proud of her. And he wanted to kiss her.

As she laughed with unrestrained joy, he could feel himself getting pulled into her orbit, trapped by the whirling feeling she created in his heart and his head.

I will not fall for this woman, he told himself. For her sake and mine, I will *not*.

Chapter Seven

Richard Maguire had many claims to fame and he liked to remind himself of these strengths when he felt off his game.

Harvard and Wharton. CEO of a multi-national company. Soon to be engaged to a Smithie if things with Penelope kept apace. His handicap on the links was under ten and sinking. And he was still able to wear the tuxedo he'd had in high school. Comfortably.

But his most useful attribute? He was a very good chess player.

So his sister Madeline's silly little offensive was not going to be a problem.

Feeling more satisfied with himself, Richard pulled into his driveway, noting it was five o'clock sharp. He steered his Lexus back to the garages and reviewed the evening ahead. Penelope had gone home to change at her father's and she and the other guests would be arriving in an hour.

Perfect. A perfect afternoon and a perfect night to look forward to.

He was very pleased with the way the golfing had gone today and things were looking up. Over eighteen holes, he'd been able to make some more progress with the President of Organi-Foods. If all things fell into place, the acquisition of that company by Value Shop Supermarkets would go forward. Provided that Richard's conservative board got with the program.

Barker, his chairman, was a big problem. And that was why Madeline had to be kept from voting. The last thing Richard needed was another wild card at the table when he was trying to get this acquisition passed by the trustees. Madeline simply wouldn't understand the issues or how critical it was to expand in this marketplace. For God's sake, she'd no doubt be dumb enough to vote against the plan just to spite him.

Richard got out of his sedan and walked into his house through the kitchen. As he looked over the catering staff for the evening's party, he found them appropriately rushed and so he headed for his bedroom. He was moving at a clip, going toward the grand staircase when he stopped dead in the foyer.

From out of the bank of windows ahead, he saw Madeline and that chef on the terrace. The guy was facing away from the house and had his shirt off and…holy hell, he had a *tattoo* all down his spine.

Except it wasn't that obscene marking that truly worried Richard. The real problem was Madeline. His sister was staring at the man like he was a god.

This was not happening. This whole thing…Was. Not. Happening.

Madeline was docile, meek, soft. For all the muscle on

her frame, she had cotton balls in her heart. Where the hell was this backbone of hers coming from?

Richard shook his head and realized he'd forgotten the essential dynamic: she wasn't the one who wanted to make a change in the trust.

If Madeline happened to take control, she could not only vote her shares, she could sell them for cash…and invest in all kinds of harebrained schemes. Like French restaurants in New York City owned by chefs who had tattoos.

Abruptly, Spike glanced over his shoulder, as if he'd sensed he was being watched. His eyes narrowed and he pegged Richard with a hard look, right through the window.

Richard smiled and nodded, then jogged up the stairs. When he got to his bedroom, he went to the phone on his desk. His lawyer answered her cell on the first ring with a sharp, ready voice. She was no doubt still at her office in Manhattan even though it was late on the Saturday afternoon of Memorial Day weekend.

Richard kicked off his loafers. "I want you to do a background check on someone."

"I make no promises. Name?" The woman talked like a teletype machine. And was just about as polite.

"Michael Moriarty. Goes by Spike." Richard pulled open his desk drawer and took out a piece of paper. "I've got his social security number."

"Give it to me."

Richard read off the page then slipped the thing back into the desk. "I want to know everything about this guy."

"An incomplete report is useless." Her strident tone of voice suggested he'd get details down to Moriarty's shoe size and first grade teacher. "You will hear from me in twenty-four hours."

"And I have disconcerting news." He explained the situation with Madeline's trust. "I've got to retain control of those shares if the takeover of Organi-Foods is to go through. I need to be the big elephant in the room with the largest block of votes because that damned board is so conservative. I've got enough stuffed shirts at that table. I don't want to have a loose cannon like her there with them."

"If I recall, the provisions of the trust will permit you to raise a fiduciary fitness argument on the basis of business incompetence. If you can persuade a judge that she cannot properly steward the trust's resources, she can be prevented from taking control."

"I'm well aware of that and I expect you to start working on it. And I want that information on Moriarty. He's the one behind all this, a chef looking to expand his restaurant with my sister's money. Need I say more?"

Richard ended the call and picked up his loafers.

Going through Moriarty's things last night had been the work of a moment and Richard was quite pleased by how well he'd done the job. No way the man would know someone had been in his room.

The purpose behind the search had actually been for drugs. The last thing Richard needed was an overdose or some horrible crime of passion thing going down at the Maguire compound. Chefs, even well-trained French ones, didn't necessarily follow the law. Richard had heard stories coming out of Manhattan. *Kitchen Confidential* indeed.

While he'd been going through the wallet he'd found, he'd memorized Moriarty's social security number and had written it down later only on a lark. But now that he knew Spike's motivation? How useful those nine digits had proven to be.

Richard smiled. Yes, he was a very fine chess player.

He threw open his walk-in closet, put his shoes back where they belonged, and then gazed with satisfaction at all the clothes lined up so neatly on matching wood and brass hangers. He changed into a seersucker suit and slipped a red bow tie around his neck.

Tonight, Madeline would meet Charles Barker, the board chairman, and Charles would be unimpressed because Madeline was unimpressive as women went: she never dressed like anything and had no great intellect when it came to things other than sports. And not even her athletic knowledge was relevant because sailboat racing was so obscure.

During her meeting with Barker, Madeline would become flustered because that was what she did when she was out of her comfort zone. And she would realize that she had no business being on the board. Then she would back down and sign the papers, allowing Richard to retain control.

Provided he could get her backbone out of the picture.

Fortunately, Michael "Spike" Moriarty looked like the kind of man who would have some secrets to hide.

Everything was going to be fine.

Richard squared up his bow tie and headed out. Only to pause at the door.

With a quick stride, he went back to the phone on his desk and dialed. As it rang, he constructed the voice-mail message he would leave, because there would be no answer. Not on a long weekend when everyone who was anyone was out of Manhattan.

His sister Amelia's voice was a surprise. "Hello?" she said.

"Amelia, you're home."

"Richard." She took a deep breath. "How are you?"

"I expected you to be out of the city."

"I was supposed to have been. But my plans changed."

"Good. I want you to come out to Greenwich. You shouldn't be alone on a holiday weekend."

There was a long pause. "You haven't invited me out in a while."

"Your social life is the stuff of a Candace Bushnell novel. When are you ever free?" He looked out the window and made a note that the pear trees needed to be fertilized. "So you'll come?"

"Actually…I wouldn't mind a change of scenery. I'll be there first thing tomorrow."

When Richard hung up, he was smiling. Amelia was a good sister. Astonishingly attractive, for one thing, and she was finally losing that edge of hers, mellowing out, becoming involved in appropriate things down in the city like the Brooklyn Zoo and the Met and MOMA.

She also trusted that he'd take care of the business.

When their father had died, no restrictions had been set up for Amelia or Richard's inheritances because, unlike Madeline, they'd been over twenty-one—the true age of majority in their father's eyes. Almost immediately, Amelia had executed a durable power of attorney over her shares, granting Richard the right to vote them. In return, he gave her a generous allowance and invested the rest of her holdings wisely. To her credit, she was grateful to him and she had reason to be. In spite of her spending, she was richer now than she'd been just after she'd gotten her money.

So he didn't worry about her. In fact, she was an asset. Particularly in a situation like this.

Amelia would show up at the house and Madeline would kick right into orbit: it was clear she was half in love with Spike, and if there was one sure way to drive a wedge between Madeline and a man, it was Amelia.

Yes…life was just like chess. It was all a matter of lining up the pieces and letting the play commence.

An hour or so later, Spike could not take his eyes off of Mad.

Which wasn't exactly a newsflash.

In the midst of a room full of talking people, she was the only one he saw, and not just because she was standing right next to him. She was wearing the same black knit dress she'd had on at Sean's and she looked better than ever in it, the simple lines showing off her body's strength as well as its curves. Her hair was flowing down her back and he had to put his free hand in his pocket to keep from brushing over the dark waves.

Strange, though. She honestly had no idea that she was beautiful. Even as all the men looked at her, lingered around her, tried to get up the nerve to talk to her, she didn't seem to notice. The disassociation made him angry on her behalf. How many times must she have been browbeaten by the men in her family to be so removed from how attractive she was?

"Here comes Richard," she murmured, taking a sip of her Chardonnay.

Spike glanced to the right and didn't like the look in the man's eyes as the guy approached. Her half brother was way too pleased with himself. And there was someone behind him.

Richard stopped in front of Mad. "Madeline, I'd like to introduce you to the chairman of my board, Charles Barker."

Now that guy is right out of central casting, Spike

thought. Barker was total chairman material: white haired with wire-rimmed glasses and all suited up in black pin-stripes even though it was summer. His eyes were as sharp as his screaming red power tie.

Mad offered her hand. "I'm pleased to meet you, Mr. Barker."

"Call me Charles." The smile was quick. So was the shake. "I understand you sail. Do you know my son, Charles? He races off Newport."

Mad's eyes flared. "You're Chuck Barker's father?"

"I am." Now Barker smiled widely. "You've heard of him?"

"Chuckie's a fabulous helmsman! Were you on shore when he and his team won last year's Mem Day relay off Newport?"

Barker let out a guffaw that was a total surprise. And then positively glowed with pride. "I was. We have a house there."

"God, I thought Chuckie was going to capsize. I really did. But he held his line. He's really going to be a great competitor one day."

As the two of them kept on chatting, Spike glanced at Richard. The guy was watching the exchange, like he couldn't wait to jump in and break it up.

"So what are you preparing for now?" Barker asked Mad.

"She wants to join our board," Richard drawled. "In her spare time."

The chairman cocked an eyebrow. "That's a shift from sailing."

Mad nodded. "It is. But I'm interested in the company."

Barker shook his head. "Well, there's a lot of moving parts to it. Lot of tedium, too. The monthly financials alone are the size of the phone book."

Richard smiled. "I told her that."

When? Spike wondered. Not that he'd heard.

Barker put his hand on Mad's shoulder. "I can't imagine it's as exciting as what you do for a living." He glanced at Richard. "Surely you can continue to free her up to enjoy the sea?"

Richard nodded gravely. "That's the best thing for everyone. And I know Madeline wouldn't want to slow things down at the top while she tries to get up to speed."

Mad smiled, nice and tight. "I think you'll be surprised at how fast I can go."

Charles laughed. "Oh, that we know. I saw how you and Alex Moorehouse handled the last America's Cup. Amazing! But listen, forget about the Corporate America stuff and concentrate on those boats. Your country needs you! We've got to keep that trophy away from the Aussies."

Mad opened her mouth, but someone came up to Barker and introduced himself. As the chairman turned away, Richard leaned in and said, "Charles is right. Stick with what you know, Madeline. It'll be a much better result for you."

Her half brother walked off into the crowd.

As Mad watched him, her expression was one of calculation rather than hurt. "He's going to make a case that I'm not competent enough to vote my shares and he's going to bring Barker in on it." She glanced at Spike. "Thank God for Mick Rhodes. That's all I've got to say."

They went in for dinner shortly thereafter and Spike actually enjoyed talking to the grande dame he was seated next to. Naturally, though, he kept staring across the table at Mad, watching her push her food around and smile with reserve at the men on either side of her. With the candlelight flickering over her face, he couldn't help but think about kissing. And what she would look like without that dress on.

As there were thunderstorms coming, the party adjourned to the library, not the terrace, for the coffee/brandy/cigar phase of things. Spike caught Mad just as she left the dining room.

"How about some air?" His voice was way too husky. And he tried not to think about why he wanted to get her away from the party…knew damn well that it was because he wanted to kiss her again even though that was a stupid idea.

She smiled at him. "Let's go."

The easy reply told him she had no idea what was on his mind. Which was good. It reminded him that he had no business thinking as he did.

They walked out onto the terrace then kept going, wandering on to the lawn, drifting down away from the house. The currents in the soft summer evening carried the scents of both the blooming garden and the coming storm. Fireflies danced and flirted all around, their company far more appealing than that of the partygoers indoors.

More intimate, too.

"This stuff with Richard," Mad said, "it makes me think."

"Can I just say, you're doing great with him."

"You know…I agree. And it makes me remember other challenges, other things that I thought I couldn't handle."

Mad walked a little ahead of him and his eyes clung to the movement of her hips. When she stopped abruptly, he let himself come up right against her until he pressed his body into the back of hers. It wasn't a conscious decision. It was instinct.

As he molded himself to her, she inhaled sharply.

Immediately he eased off and gave her some space. "Sorry."

Her head turned so he saw her profile over her shoulder. She was so beautiful in the rich summer night, he thought. The kind of woman a man never forgot.

Good Lord, he wanted her.

"Have you ever fallen into the ocean?" she murmured.

Spike pushed his hand through his hair. Well, if that wasn't a change in subject from what was on his mind. "Ah, no. I haven't."

"I have. In the middle of a storm. With nothing more than a parka, a slicker and a PFD on." His heart dropped, even though her voice was utterly level as she spoke. "The boat took off without me. I watched it disappear."

Spike stopped breathing, imagining her lost. Alone. In the vast sea. His gut clenched.

"You know what I did?" she said.

"What?" he whispered. Oh, God…

"I activated my GPS, turned on my flasher and waited."

Spike's breath eased. "Smart."

"I was found eight hours later."

Holy… Eight hours? In a storm? "*Mad.*"

"I thought I was dead. I really did. And after I got through the fear of it all, I was okay with the dying…because I kind of figured I'd done what I wanted to. I mean, I'd found the thing I loved to do above all others and I'd excelled at my sailing and my competing. I had lived the way I wanted."

Spike swallowed. "How long ago did this happen?"

"Two months."

Spike cursed.

Her eyes flipped up to his. "I saw you watching me during dinner."

Whoa. And to think he'd assumed his blushing days were long over. "I, ah…"

"You kept looking at me. Every time I glanced over the table, you were staring. You were focused on my lips, weren't you."

He cleared his throat. Okay, so maybe she had known what he was thinking of when he asked her to go for a walk. "Mad, I—"

"I want to be your lover. Tonight."

Spike's body instantly shot into the stratosphere. As their eyes held fast over her shoulder, he read everything in her face: the decision, the conviction…the wanting.

And he wasn't going to turn away from her. Even though he in no way deserved her and she didn't know the particulars of the *why* in that, he was not going to walk away.

Because he couldn't.

He moved in closer, bringing his chest to her back again, sinking his hips into her. He moved her long, dark hair out of the way, balling it into his hungry fist. Then he leaned down, pressed his lips to her neck and growled, "Say that again."

She swayed. "I want to be your lover."

"When," he prompted, biting at her throat then kissing what he'd taken between his teeth. He was gentle…but not too gentle.

"Tonight…"

He reached around and swept his hand up her neck, capturing her jaw. He moved his thumb back and forth over her lower lip. "How about…right now?"

He twisted her head around, tilted it back and kissed her long and slow. As her body arched back against his own, he braced his weight, holding her up.

"Let's go to my bedroom," he said roughly against her

mouth. Then he pressed his tongue between her lips. She met the thrust with one of her own and he moaned.

Man, much more of this and he was going to have her on the grass...which was not only indecent, but ungentlemanly.

"There's something you need to know," she murmured.

"What?" He slid his hand lower, going between her breasts, down over her stomach and lower...until he brushed the tops of her thighs.

"I'm a virgin."

Spike froze.

The first thing that went through his mind was that a man like him shouldn't take something so special from a woman like Madeline Maguire. But then that conviction was followed immediately by something even more powerful: Let me be the one. The only one for her. Ever.

The idea was so outrageous and so deep, he stunned himself into silence and had to release her. He took a step back. And then another.

What the hell was he thinking? Madeline Maguire was not the sort of woman you took to bed for a one-nighter. Or even a one-weekender. So he should be ashamed of himself at any rate. But add to all that the fact that it would be her first time?

And that she didn't know about his past?

This could not happen, he thought, appalled at himself. As much as he wanted it to, they just could not be together.

Okay, so maybe she could have been less blunt, Mad thought. Although given the horror on Spike's face, couching the announcement in euphemisms wouldn't have made any difference.

As he just stared at her, all she could do was stare back. Until she couldn't stand the silence a second longer.

"Look, I'm not expecting more than this weekend, Spike. I just wanted to be up-front. So you weren't surprised when we…"

He took yet another step away. Boy, if he kept that up, he was going to be over the state line and back in New York soon.

"Yeah, Mad…I don't know."

She ignored the stabbing sensation in her chest and looked at the sky. Which was far better than watching him inch away like she was radioactive. "It shouldn't change anything. I'm an adult. So are you. And this isn't the turn of the century."

Lightning flashed on the horizon.

"Why me?" he said softly.

"Why wouldn't it be you?" Thunder crept through the night, a slow rolling bass. "I want you."

He coughed a little as if she'd embarrassed him. "Mad…I don't…"

She forced a laugh. "You know what? It's okay. I can understand you not wanting to get tangled in something messy."

"It's just—I shouldn't be your first. That's all."

Narrowing her eyes, she shook her head. "Hold up. If you don't want to be with me, fine. But don't throw that chivalry thing into the mix, okay? I'm perfectly capable of deciding who I want."

His voice grew hard. "There are things you don't know about me."

Mad put her hands on her hips and glared at him. Then she said, "Red."

He frowned. "Excuse me?"

"My favorite color is red. Did you know that? And I'm an Aries. April fourth is my birthday. Also, I had my tonsils out when I was two. You know any of that?"

Anger flashed in his eyes. "Don't patronize me."

"I'm not! My point is, neither one of us knows a great deal about the other." She threw her hands up. "And the not knowing should probably matter. Except with you...I don't seem to care so much. Richard is right. I don't have good luck with men. And that's why... Look, you're here with me now and I want to be with you and that's enough for me. I don't care about your past or what I may not know about you. I like who you are now. I like that you over-tipped the waitress this morning...and I love that crazy bike...and I'm thrilled you don't care that I'm a strong swimmer...and—"

Something wet hit her face. A rain drop. When she tilted her head back, another hit her cheek.

"God, I do go on, don't I," she muttered, very aware that he was saying nothing. "Come on, let's go inside before the storm hits us."

When she headed for the house, he walked behind her. But unlike the trip out, she couldn't feel the heat of his eyes on her body anymore.

By the time they hit the terrace, the rain was steady.

Mad had no intention of going back to the party. There was no way she could face that pressure cooker. And as she went up the stairs, he followed as if he felt the same way. Just before they got to the second floor, a jagged streak of lightning shot out of the sky and a split second later there was a mighty roar.

"Will your bike be okay?" she asked as they stepped off into the hallway.

"I heard the storm was coming so I moved Bette into the garage. The butler was cool about it."

"Oh, good." She lifted her hand casually, but she had to

work at it. The thing felt like it weighed a hundred pounds. "So…'night."

"Good night, Mad."

She walked down the hall, knowing he wasn't going to stop her.

Inside her bedroom, the window she'd opened that morning was still raised so the storm was blowing the drapes out and the sill was wet. She cleaned up the water, but left the thing open. Now that she was no longer a child, she loved thunderstorms.

Would have loved to have watched this one with Spike from her bed.

God, she felt wretched. Absolutely wretched.

After a quick shower, she put a long T-shirt on and slid between the covers. Curling over onto her side, she stared out at the night. The lightning was intensifying, flashing across the sky. Thunder shook the house. Rain lashed down the windows.

She was going to have to dry off the sill again.

But she would do that later. She closed her eyes and listened to the storm…and drifted into a lonely sleep.

Chapter Eight

Sometime much later, Mad felt something brush against her hip. Something warm. Slow. Heavy. A hand?

She jerked just as Spike's voice whispered in her ear, "It's just me."

"What are you—" When she tried to roll over, she came flush to his hard body. And he was in her bed, not just on top of the covers—she could feel the T-shirt he had on and those nylon sweats.

His hips moved, a surge that brought his erection against the back of her thigh. As she groaned at the heat that poured through her, his hand slipped underneath her shirt, dipped into her waist and moved down across her stomach. She arched involuntarily, her head coming back against his shoulder.

He kissed her neck. "Do you have any protection?"

Surprise had her eyes widening. Okay…this was not a

dream, evidently. Because what kind of fantasy had the lovers talking about condoms?

She twisted her head and looked at him. Had he really come to... Well, yes, he had. The answer was in his glowing eyes.

"What changed your mind?" she whispered.

He eased away just enough so she could roll over on to her back. Then he brushed a strand of hair from her face and kissed her lightly on the mouth. His voice was quiet in the darkness, the voice of a lover.

"I thought about something I told your captain, Alex, a couple of months ago. I reminded him that warmth in this life is so very rare...and that when you find it, you need to revel in it." Spike kissed her shoulder. Then her throat. Then her jawline. "I want you so badly I can't sleep from the burn. And if the present is enough for you, then tonight, let's be together. If you still—"

"Yes. Yes..."

His hand swept up until it was just under her breasts, but then he paused. "Mad, I need you to know that I don't want to hurt you."

"It won't last long," she murmured, imagining where they were going to end up. Wanting it so dearly she almost wept.

"I'm not just talking about the...sex part."

She laid her palm on his face. "I know. But I heard what you said this morning. I know you're not looking for long-term."

"I wish I were different. I wish...a lot of things were different." He kissed her softly, drawing his palm in circles on her rib cage. "But I'm really glad we're here tonight."

She stroked her way up his back, reveling in his strength. His muscles were thick at his shoulders, his spine a graceful line under his skin. She imagined the tattoo under her fingers.

We need a little light, she decided. With a quick move, she leaned to the right and clicked on the lamp.

"I want to see you," she said as she rearranged herself under him.

He flushed. "Ah, Mad...before this goes too far, do you have something? I would have stopped by a store this morning if I'd known we would be...like this."

"Oh, um...no. I don't."

His hand stopped moving and his chest expanded and contracted. Then he resumed his gentle exploration. "That's okay. We can do other things. We don't—"

"You don't need to worry about it, assuming you're clean. I've never been with anyone and you can't get me pregnant."

"I—ah, you're on the pill?"

"I don't get my period because of my physical training schedule." Okay, now she was blushing.

Spike shifted back and looked at her. "Mad...that's not good for you, is it?"

"It happens to female athletes sometimes. And I don't plan on being like this forever. When I'm no longer competing at the elite sailing level, I'll increase my food intake, decrease the exercise and it'll come back."

Spike frowned at her as if she'd scrambled him a little and she felt something cold land in her gut. She'd never really thought not getting a period was odd because it wasn't all that uncommon among the women she knew. But with the way he was looking at her now, it was as if he hadn't come across someone like her before.

"So...I'm fine," she prompted. "What about you?"

JESSICA BIRD 129

He rubbed his face, like there were things he wanted to say but he was biting his tongue. "I've always been careful. Never without a condom. Plus I had a physical six months ago. I was clean then and I haven't been with anyone since."

"So kiss me." She reached up and touched his face. "Spike, I'm fine. Don't worry about it. Kiss me...."

He hesitated and she thought for a moment he was going to use his mouth for talking. But then his head came down and his lips were soft on hers. He kissed her for so long, his tongue lazy and slow in her mouth, that she began to wonder whether they were going to end up doing anything else. Which, considering the way his lips moved over hers, was no great sacrifice.

But then he slowly pushed up her shirt so the cotton pooled at her collarbone.

"Oh... Mad..." he whispered. "You're perfect."

His hand traveled up over her rib cage and cupped one of her breasts lightly. As he gently learned her contours, his head dipped down and found her neck...then went lower until his mouth closed over her nipple. As he sucked and kissed, she grabbed on to his head, urging him closer, wanting more, wanting it all.

When he slid her panties down, she didn't really notice. But as soon as his hand skimmed over her thighs and dipped between them, she jerked.

"This okay?" he said hoarsely, pulling back.

"Yes...oh, yes. Just...surprised."

When he touched her heat, it was so softly she barely knew what he was doing. What she registered instead was the way he shuddered with an erotic little spasm, his whole body trembling, his hips surging.

"Mad," he whispered. "Oh...*Mad.*"

The rest of what he said was lost as he kissed her and touched her with sensual care, knowing exactly what felt good.

She pushed her hands between their bodies, reaching for his hips, wanting him to know the same heat and spiraling urgency. But he held her hands away from his arousal.

"No, don't touch me."

"Why—"

"I need to stay in control. This has to be good for you." His lips came down on hers and he stroked her core once again. "You're so soft here. You make me…crazy."

His body was tight all over, except for when he shivered, and the more he pleasured her with his hand, the more they both became aroused. And she knew exactly how much he wanted her. It was in his parted lips, the flush on his cheeks, his rapt breathlessness, his straining muscles…but most of all it was in the reverent, greedy way his yellow eyes looked at her.

Abruptly, he changed his touch, demanding, driving. She grabbed on to his shoulders and gasped, kicking her head back. She was swept away in him, by him, the heat growing and growing.

"I want you to fly for me," he said in her ear, his voice a thrilling rasp. "Let yourself go. I promise I'll hold you. But fly for me, Madeline. I need it. I need to see it."

When she shattered apart, he was there, whispering to her, telling her she was beautiful, riding out the wave with her then easing her down.

She buried her face in his chest as her heart began to slow, feeling an absurd urge to cry. Closer…she wanted to be closer to him. She curled into his body and tried to push her knee between his legs, but he held her in place. And that was when she realized he was retreating from her though he hadn't gone anywhere.

She looked up at him. "You want to stop now, don't you?"

His eyes roamed around her face and then he smiled a little. "Brace yourself, I'm about to be unmanly."

"Not possible. You're as manly as they come."

"I'm scared."

Her breath caught. "Of what?"

There was a pause and then his hand swept down her side, over her hip and to the apex of her thighs.

"Open for me, Mad."

She let her legs relax and then he was touching her again. With a slow gentle push, he dipped inside of her for the first time. She shifted to accommodate his hand, tilting her hips up as he went farther and farther…until he stopped and cursed softly.

"Mad, there's no way this isn't going to hurt you."

"I'll be fine." It would be over quickly and then on the other side there would be something beautiful waiting for both of them. "I'm not worried."

"Yeah, well, I am. I don't know if I can…do this." He cleared his throat. "I want you, but I'm not sure what's going to happen if I know I have to hurt you. I'm liable to lose my…you know."

"You are so adorable right now." She slid her arm around his waist and swept her hand up to his heavy shoulders. She was surprised once again at how smooth and warm his skin was. "Spike—"

"Michael."

"What?"

"My real name is Michael. You don't have to use it. I just…wanted you to know."

"Michael." She smiled. "Where did the Spike come from? Your hair?"

His eyes grew grim. "It was given to me. By…friends."

She eased her palm down his back, wondering about his friends, wondering about where he'd gotten his tattoo, wondering… She knew so few details about his life, though she knew the essence of him very well.

"Michael," she murmured. "I like that. So, Michael, kiss me. Stop thinking and kiss me."

"You aren't afraid, are you?"

"No."

His eyes became so serious the color of them seemed to darken. "You…are amazing."

With a powerful surge, he pulled his shirt off and pitched the thing carelessly to the ground. Then he stretched out on top of her, drawing her arms up over her head. After he'd settled into the cradle of her hips, he began to move in a sinuous pump. As she cried out from the friction, he groaned and let her hands go then dropped his head into the crook of her neck. Through the thin nylon of his sweats, she could feel his arousal sliding, probing. She threw her knees wide.

"Mad…"

He kissed her hard and they went a little wild as she wrapped her legs around his hips and gripped his shoulders with her nails. He didn't seem to mind how much she was holding on to him or the way she'd latched on to his lower body. Quite the opposite. He was positively growling into her mouth.

Without warning, he pulled away and stood up. Turning his back to her, he drew the sweatpants off then held them over his hips as he got back onto the bed. She was confused until she realized he was shielding himself from her, not letting her catch a glimpse of the front of him.

As he found his way back to her body, he threw the sweats aside and came down on top of her. His naked skin against hers was a stinging pleasure, almost too much to handle. But she wanted to know what he looked like.

She pushed him back. "Let me see you. All of you."

There was a pause.

"Spike, I want to see you. Now."

He slowly eased off her and rose up onto his knees. Mad's eyes widened as she understood what he hadn't wanted her to know. He was...very well endowed.

"We don't have to," he said, covering himself with his palms.

She shook her head and moved his hands away. "I don't want to stop."

"Mad...I'll be careful."

"I know you will. But first..." She reached out and touched him.

His body shuddered all over, his breath sucking into his lungs with a hiss, his head falling back. She looked at the male glory of him, from his thick thighs to his magnificent sex to the planes of his stomach...up farther to his pectorals and his shoulders...to his throat and the hard point of his chin, which was all she could see of his face.

She stroked him and learned his maleness, all of it, but he didn't let her explore for long.

His voice was hoarse, a bumpy rasp, as he lay down on top of her again. "No more of that. You take me so high, so fast..."

She felt him shift to the side and one of his hands disappeared between their hips. There was a blunt, silken brush against her, and the knowledge of what it was made her tremble with arousal. He entered with an aching, un-hurried nudge.

Spike broke out in a sweat and the heat that bloomed over every inch of him seeped into her. His muscles were absolutely rigid as he moved forward little by little, going so very carefully. As her body stretched to accommodate him, he found a shallow rhythm of rocking and she followed along.

Pleasure began to rise and she nipped his shoulder with her teeth while angling her hips up.

"Now," she whispered. "Do it now."

He stuck with speed. With one sharp surge of his lower body, he broke past the breach, but went no farther.

Pain flared, red hot, and she tightened all over, gasping. Instinctually she squeezed at his hips, and pushed against his shoulders, yet she hoped he wouldn't move.

"I'll pull out," he said in a rush.

"No…just…wait a minute, okay? I need to relax."

Spike stayed perfectly still, not even breathing.

Her tension eased as the discomfort passed. And then she was aware of him, so unnaturally quiet and unmoving, yet joined with her.

Abruptly, the presence of him seemed very right.

More, she thought. I want more.

Spike was grimacing in sympathy, still horrified to have heard her gasp and felt her body stiffen under his.

It was totally unfair, that he should only feel the pleasure of her tight hold while she bore the hurt of them coming together. And he would have taken the pain from her if he could have, born it a hundred times over to spare her.

"I'm sorry," he said. "I really think I should—"

She held him in place by the shoulders and shifted under him. The friction was so delicious he groaned and when she arched beneath him again, she drew him farther inside.

Her eyes were clear and sensually curious as she smiled. "Don't stop now. The hard part's over."

At that moment, staring down into her face, his body pressed against hers, penetrating hers, Spike felt his whole life change. Suddenly, inexplicably, everything was different. Which he supposed was what happened when you were struck by lightning.

Or…love.

Oh, no, he thought. How was it possible? No, he couldn't…

Well, at least he knew why it might have happened. It was her courage and her strength and the way she felt beneath him right now. It was her mind and her smile and the very scent of her. It was all the things he knew of her and all the things he wanted to discover about her. And, yeah, though it made him a total Neanderthal and he would have adored her anyway, the fact that he was the only man to be where he was just laid him out flat.

"Spike?" Her brows flickered in worry. "Is this…okay for you?"

"No, it's not okay. It's…everything." He kissed her deeply, joining them in another way, tongue to tongue.

Using his hips, he moved deeper and deeper, following a back-and-forth motion to ease his way, stretching her gently. She was all tight satin around him, so smooth and perfect he ground his molars. And though he wanted nothing more than to let loose and turn into a raw animal, though the base of his skull was screaming for him to go wild and pump against her until both of them exploded, the primal instinct was easy to ignore.

Because she was precious.

When they were fully together, joined pelvis to pelvis, he gathered her up, scooping his arms under her and holding her tight. With other women he'd had sex with, he hadn't particularly cared how close they got during the act. But as he eased off the choke hold on his body a little, so he could start the pace that would take Mad and him to heaven, he wanted her right in his face. He wanted to share the moment with her from head to toe. He wanted to look into her eyes.

And he did. The whole time.

It didn't take long before the smooth motion of their bodies carried him so far away that he lost his mind. And she was with him on the journey, clutching at his lower back, holding him tight, digging her nails into him. He felt her release, heard her cry muffled in his shoulder, and then the pleasure was too much. He pulled out quickly and spilled himself between their bellies, shuddering and bucking.

When he found his breath again, he rolled on to his side and took her with him, easing one thigh between her legs and cradling her against his chest.

Eventually, she pulled back a little and looked at him. The smile on her face and the glow in her eyes made his heart pole-vault up into his throat.

Do not say something stupid, he thought.

Oh, man…he wanted to. He wanted to blurt out three little words he couldn't possibly mean.

"You all right?" he asked.

"Yes." She kissed his jawline. "You're wonderful."

"No, that was all you. Every bit of it. I'm…nothing

special." He shifted his hips back. Separating their bodies felt all wrong, but he got out of bed anyway. "Come with me. I want to wash you."

He held out his hand and when she took his palm, he couldn't resist drawing her against him for a moment. Then they went into the bathroom together, lazy, relaxed, all in the afterglow. As she turned the lights on and dimmed them, he started the shower and waited with his hand under the spray for the warmth to come.

It wasn't until she brushed by him to step into the steam that he saw the blood on the inside of her thighs. He glanced down his body, saw more on himself, and felt like passing out.

"Spike, stop it. You know I'm fine." She pulled at him. "Come on, get in with me."

He kissed her then, with an intensity that came from the soul. And when he pulled back, his eyes were stinging a little so he hid them from her by getting under the water. God...the idea he'd made her bleed in that way shook him so badly he was nauseous.

He washed her carefully, and when she took the hand towel and insisted on returning the favor, all he could do was lean back against the tile and let her go where she pleased.

When they were back in bed, he snuggled in close to her, loving her body against his own.

There was a long silence. "Mad?"

"Yes?"

He cleared his throat, wanting to talk. Because if he didn't let some of what he was thinking out, his head was going to unhinge like a fricking Pez dispenser.

Except when he opened his mouth, there was nothing... nothing he could really say at any rate. So he kissed her, feeling inadequate.

"Nothing. Just… I think you're beautiful."

When he would have pulled away, she snuck her hands around his neck and held him against her mouth. As her tongue licked into him, he felt his body thicken in a rush. He moved his lower body back, not wanting her to feel the least bit pressured. But then her hand found his arousal.

"So soon?" she said with a husky laugh.

"Um…yeah, but we don't—" She stroked him and he sucked a breath in through his teeth.

"You're going to let me touch you this time," she said.

"Are you sure you're ready to…"

She rolled him over and moved down his body. "I have an idea. Why don't I be in control for a little while?"

Spike gasped at what she did next, his hands tangling in her hair, his hips surging. Closing his eyes, he gave himself to her with no boundaries at all.

Chapter Nine

Mad woke up in tangled sheets, her face buried in a pillow that smelled like Spike's aftershave. As she stretched, her body sent back reminders that she'd done something different during the night. Three times.

She smiled and wished her lover were next to her, but Spike had insisted on leaving just as the dawn arrived. It was endearing that a man who looked so unconventional was all worried about someone finding out they'd spent the night together.

And what a night.

Boy, given her dating past, she never would have guessed that when she finally had sex it would be such a beautiful, moving experience. But it had been, with all the right things done and said and felt. Spike had made it special for her in each touch and whisper, every kiss and heartbeat. And it had been special for him, too. She'd seen it in his eyes.

Memories of them together came to her, warmed her, made her restless. He'd been so careful not to release when they were joined, always breaking the connection before his body reached its pinnacle. In the light of day, she was glad because it showed how scrupulous he was. Even though the precaution was unnecessary.

Mad frowned. Pushing the covers down her body, she looked at her stomach. She was so lean and so strong, she could see each one of her individual abdominal muscles. Passing her hand over her belly, she pictured herself going soft. Getting round. Growing big.

Carrying a child.

She splayed her hand out. What would that feel like?

And, yes, the baby in this hypothetical had yellow eyes.

Mad groaned and stood up. She'd made love for the first time last night and she was already thinking about pregnancy? For heaven's sake, she didn't have the kind of lifestyle for that sort of thing.

Or the man for it, either. Just because she and Spike had shared something wonderful, didn't change the fact that they were going their separate ways. Even if he magically decided he wanted a woman in his life, her sailing schedule was a crusher and he wasn't going to quit his chef job just to follow her around the globe.

They had this one weekend together, this one very special weekend that she would cherish always....

God, her chest hurt.

And as she stepped into the shower the ache got worse. She couldn't help fantasizing about a future that would never happen.

Picking up a bar of soap, which she remembered using on Spike's body, she started to wash herself. When she ran the thing over her lower belly she stopped, a flash of fear snaking through her. Not getting a period had always seemed like such a relief; she never missed the hassle or the discomfort. And it was great to wake up every morning knowing she was going to feel the same as the day before because there was none of that monthly mood swing thing.

Except what if it never came back? Exactly what kind of gamble was she taking with her body?

She thought of Spike, worshiping her with his hands, his mouth…the most intimate part of himself. She'd never given much thought about being a woman before. She was an athlete first and foremost, a competitor. But last night, underneath him, on top of him, all over him, she'd felt very female.

And she'd loved it.

As Spike stepped out of his guest room, he looked down the long hall. He wasn't sure what the protocol was, but he was definitely knocking on Mad's door before he went down for breakfast. And if the two of them walking into that sunroom together was a problem, he'd just have to give their audience a big whatever.

He needed to see Mad.

While heading down to her room, he figured he should have been in rough shape because he'd been up all night watching her sleep. Instead, the hour's shut-eye in his own bed and the shower he'd just had was all it took to totally revive him. He was wired in this best kind of way, totally alive.

He came up to her door and took a deep breath, telling his body that now was not the time for anything remotely sexual. Except as he knocked, all he could think about was how they'd spent the hours in her bed and he was instantly primed. Again.

When there was no answer, he went downstairs. The sunroom where the family ate breakfast was in an alcove off the dining room, and as he stepped inside the bright little space, his eyes adjusted and he grinned like an idiot. Mad was sitting in a ray of sunshine, a coffee cup in her hands. The moment she saw him, she blushed and offered him a slow, secret smile.

"You look well rested," Richard muttered while flipping his *New York Times* around with a crack.

Spike took the seat next to Mad. "It's the country air. And all the exercise I've been getting."

As Mad's cheeks got even rosier, Spike had to force himself not to take her hand and give it a squeeze.

He was still looking at her when a plate of poached eggs on toast materialized in front of him. God, he was ravenous. Capable of eating thirds. He tucked into the breakfast with the enthusiasm of his teenage years.

When he sensed Mad's gaze on him, he glanced over at her. She was staring at his hands on his silverware and he knew exactly what she was thinking. To get her attention, he stroked the handle of the knife with his forefinger. As her eyes shot up to his, he deliberately licked his lower lip then bit down on it. Her coffee cup trembled and she looked away, smiling.

Richard rustled his paper again. "So now that your guard dog is here, may we discuss your trust?"

Mad stiffened. "I told you fifteen minutes ago. I told you yesterday. I'm not going to sign those papers."

"Well—" her half brother looked over the top of the business section "—something tells me you'll change your mind soon enough."

From out in the foyer, there came a fast clipping sound.

High heels, Spike thought. And they were heading this way.

The blond woman who appeared in the sunroom's doorway was an absolutely stunning creature, all Grace Kelly-esque: perfect features, perfect body, perfect long, wavy flaxen hair. She was dressed in white slacks and a pale blue blouse and had a gold chain belt around her waist. Her perfume was delicate and undoubtedly French and her aura was one of profound privilege.

Spike frowned, thinking he'd seen her before. Or maybe not. He could just be getting her mixed up with one of any number of Manhattan's A-list types. God knew there were plenty of picture-perfect blondes wearing Chanel in the Big Apple.

Whatever…whether he'd seen her in passing before or not, this had to be Amelia and he supposed Mad was right. Most men would be picking their chins off their plates at the arrival of such a high-class knockout. Except as far as Spike was concerned, Grace Kelly over there couldn't hold a candle to the woman he had held against him last night.

He glanced over at Mad. Oh, man, she was white as a sheet.

Richard peered around his paper and smiled. "There you are, Amelia."

The blonde nodded in his direction in a vague way, seeming to see only Mad. In a quiet voice, she said, "Hello, Madeline. I…didn't know you were here."

Mad barely nodded, having evidently gone rigid in her chair. "Amelia."

There was a long pause.

Richard broke the silence by tossing his section of newspaper aside. "Perhaps I'll introduce our guest, as Madeline doesn't seem to want to. This is her friend, Spike."

The guy enunciated his words hard, like he was punching the air.

Amelia's gaze shifted over. Her eyes were pale gray and lovely, but curiously flat. Kind of like fake pearls, Spike thought.

"Hello," she said.

Spike lifted a hand, but didn't much care about the introduction. His only concern was how bad Mad looked. And how long it was going to take him to get her out of the room. Because sure as hell, this arrival was an ambush of some kind.

As Amelia sat down, Richard smiled, picked up another section of the *Times* and started leafing through it. "So good to have the family back together again, isn't it?"

"If you'll excuse me," Mad said, getting to her feet, "I'm finished."

Spike stood up even though he'd only made it through half the food on his plate.

"Running away, Madeline?" Richard flipped to another page and snapped the section back into shape. "Not exactly a good quality to offer a corporate board."

Spike leaned forward, put his index finger on the top of the *Times* and dragged the thing down. The sound of the paper giving way was loud and crispy in the tense room.

"Apologize for that cheap shot," he said softly to Richard.

The other man's eyes went wide. "I beg your pardon."

"Take that crack back. Now."

"What are you, her thug?"

"If that's the way you want to see it, yeah, I am. But it would nice if you could man up and not be such a bastard to your half sister."

Mad took Spike's arm. "It's okay. Really."

"No, it's not."

"Spike. Drop it."

The only reason he broke the eye contact with Richard was that he didn't want to cause Mad any more stress. But easing off was damn hard.

Especially when Richard looked at Mad and said, "And you can't stand up for yourself, either. Just what do you think you have to offer Value Shop Supermarkets, anyway?"

Spike was about to take that paper and do something socially unacceptable with it when Mad threw her shoulders back and said calmly, "I'm going to surprise you, Richard."

"Indeed. And I'm sure Amelia would like to be surprised, too, wouldn't you? She and I just love surprises."

The blonde was sitting stock still in her chair, looking like some kind of impressionist oil painting in the sunlight and her pale clothes. "Actually, I think Madeline should be on the board," she said quietly.

Mad's head whipped around.

And so did Richard's.

The man's eyes narrowed on Amelia. "Do you." When she nodded, he said dryly, "And this is because you know so much about governing boards, of course."

"I'm on the Met's."

Richard lifted his paper up again, clearly bored. Or more likely pretending to be. "That's nonprofit. Publicly held corporations are different."

Enough of this, Spike thought. He was in a table-flipping rage on Mad's behalf and the only cure was to get away from this circus. Otherwise, he was liable to put Richard head-first into the ground.

Mad seemed to have come to the same conclusion he did

because she turned and walked out of the room. He followed, and when they got to the foyer, he pulled her to a stop.

"We should just leave. Right now. This is whacked. You don't need this."

She pulled away from him, crossing her arms over her chest. "There's nothing I'd rather do than get away."

"So let's go."

"Except Richard has a point. I run. That's what I do. I've always run away from them and that stops right now. I'm staying until the end of the weekend." Abruptly, she tilted her head and looked at him as if he were a complete stranger. "A word about my half sister. She prefers men who are polished, but she'll take anyone who catches my eye. So if you're into her, all you have to do is ask and she'll be happy to oblige, I'm sure."

Spike recoiled as if she'd slapped him.

As Mad turned her back on him, he grabbed her arm. "Oh, no you don't. You do not drop a nasty like that and get to twirl away from me."

Mad's eyes were angry, unseeing. "Let go of my arm."

He pulled her forward until she was against his body. "Is that all you have to say to me?"

They squared off nose to nose, a hostile, heated spark flaring between them.

"Maybe Richard was right," she said softly. "Maybe you are a thug. Maybe that's why you and Sean get along so well. Two street fighters who pretend to be civilized."

"How those Nikes feel on your feet right now, Madeline? Guess I'm not on that short list of people you won't run from."

As he felt her tremble in anger, he wondered what the

hell they were doing, standing in the foyer, biting at each other. How had they sunk so low so fast after last night?

He dropped her arm, held his hands up and went for the front door. "I'm sorry… I'm… Yeah, I'm out of here."

Mad felt positively ill as she heard the Harley roar to life and take off.

When the thundering din faded, she covered her face with her hands and cursed. That argument just now had been her fault. She'd goaded Spike, taken out her anger on him.

But the thing was, she'd watched when Amelia had walked into the sunroom. She'd seen him appraise her half sister. And she knew what he saw.

Amelia was even more beautiful than ever. The past four years had sharpened the woman's features and incomparable sense of style, elevating her above mere humans, like a priceless figurine on a shelf. Who wouldn't be enchanted?

Except unlike Spike, Mad knew what was underneath the fine wrapping: all that calculation, all that casual, careless cruelty that led to a desire to play with other people's emotions. If Richard was an in-your-face destructive force, Amelia was the kind that came in the back door, taking shots by stealth.

Which was the only reason the woman had supported Mad going on the corporation's board. Amelia knew that would drive Richard insane.

Mad shook herself into focus and headed for the stairs, jogging up them fast. In her room, she changed into her swimsuit and then went down to the pool. As she dove into the water and set a brutal pace, she told herself she could take it. Whatever Richard and Amelia threw at her, she could take it and live.

As for Spike? She would apologize to him, of course, but she would keep her distance. Last night…last night she'd thought she knew everything that mattered about him, that the present was enough. Now, she wished she'd known him for years because trust took time and experience and they'd had neither. So in the face of having had two men she was with leave her for Amelia, it was hard to believe Spike wouldn't do the same thing.

After all, when the *second* boyfriend of hers had met her half sister, Mad had told herself it couldn't possibly happen again—she couldn't possibly have another man she was interested in prefer Amelia. Good heavens, she'd thought back then, what were the chances of it happening twice?

Damn good, as it turned out. She'd batted two for two at getting left at the side of the road. Adding a third to the tally just didn't seem that far out of the realm of plausibility.

As Mad thought about Amelia materializing in the sunroom's doorway, looking like a queen, she recalled Spike's yellow eyes going over the woman.

The pain was so great Mad flubbed her stroke and struggled to fall back into her rhythm. Those betrayals by the two other men seemed minor if she considered what it would be like to have Spike fall into Amelia's bed. After last night, she'd be ruined if Amelia got her claws into him.

Chapter Ten

Mad climbed out of the pool an hour later. She dried herself with her towel, wrapped it around her body and then sat down on a lawn chair. The swimming had been therapeutic, clearing her mind a little, calming her emotions. Now if Spike would just let her apologize—

"I'm really pissed off at you."

Mad jumped and glanced behind her. Spike was standing a couple of yards away on the terrace and his stance made it seem as if he were facing an opponent: his feet were spread apart and his hands were planted on his hips. His eyes were as dark as yellow could get.

"You have every right to be angry," she said, shifting around and looking right at him. "I was going to come find you. I'm very sorry I jumped on you like that."

He nodded, but his posture didn't change. "Apology accepted. Now I want to know what's doing with your sister."

"Half sister."

"Whatever."

"No, the distinction matters to me." She glanced at the house, noting the many windows that were open to the morning air. She owed him more than an apology, she owed him an explanation, but she had to have some privacy. "Do you mind if we walk a little?"

"If that's what you need to talk, I'm all for it."

As he crossed the flagstone, she shoved her bare feet into her running shoes and left the laces unbound.

"You're going to trip," he said.

She bent down and made two hasty knots.

As they walked over the bright green grass to the flower beds, the sun bore down on them, the heat seeming oppressive rather than soothing.

"Amelia…" She cleared her throat. "Amelia is…"

God, she couldn't find the words.

"Come on, Mad, do you actually believe I'd make a move on her?"

She stopped and met him in the eye. "Twice. It's happened to me twice before. So when a man I…like is around my half sister, my instinct is to cut my losses. Not your fault and I'm honestly sorry."

He frowned. "How can you think I'd screw you over like that?"

"I want to trust you. I really do. It's just…seeing her this morning made me realize how little I know you. I mean, I wish we'd spent more time together. Or that I had something, some kind of context for you like more details about your life, where you've been, what you've done." As his face tightened, she cursed softly, realizing how she must be coming across. "Ah…hell. I don't mean to put this back on you again. Listen, Amelia and I and Richard, we're a bad combination and our roles are set like bricks in a wall. I'm very sorry you're tangled in it."

He went over to a group of tea roses and stared down at the fat, rainbow-vivid blooms. Then he took a seat on a marble bench and plugged his elbows into his knees.

He looked up at her, his eyes burning. "You're right. We don't know each other all that well, do we?"

She sat down beside him, the bench's stone warm against the back of her legs and her seat.

In the silence that followed, a crazy impulse took hold of her. She fought it, but ended up losing.

"There's a remedy for that whole not-knowing thing." She cleared her throat. "You could stick around. I could stick around. We could…stick around."

His gaze shifted away. When he rubbed his face, she knew with a chill that the next thing he was going to do was shake his head.

And he did. "It wouldn't work. I'm not…built for that."

Pain lanced through her chest.

But you knew this about him, she reminded herself. You knew this before you were with him. He couldn't have been any clearer in front of that café yesterday morning.

Fine, but it still murdered her.

"Mind if I ask why relationships don't interest you?" When he hesitated, she said with an edge, "Or is that too personal?"

"They're just not for me."

"Why?"

He looked her in the face. At first, the exhausted light in his eyes offended her because she assumed he was impatient with her question. But then she saw something else: pain. An achy, lonely pain.

"I wish I had a better answer for you." He stood up. "Let's go back to the house, okay?"

"Now who's running?" she whispered.

A vicious word drifted out of his mouth. But then he said, "Yeah…you're right."

He rubbed the top of his head, making his hair stand up even straighter. Then he glanced back at the mansion. As his eyes narrowed, he seemed to be tracing the lines of the massive house as if he were taking mathematical measurements.

"I'm not…" His voice drifted. "I'm really not worthy of you."

She frowned, appalled. "Spike, I don't care if you didn't grow up like I did. I'm not into money."

"I know." A shadow of a smile lifted his lips. "Although I do feel compelled to mention that your garage is bigger than the house I was raised in."

"Not my garage. My father's, then my half brother's. Never mine. And *I'd* like to point out that your bike is bigger than the bunks I sleep on."

Now he really smiled. "Touché."

But his expression drained away quickly. "If I were a different man, Mad—" He shook his head as if cutting his words off with the motion. "I have no regrets. Well, no regrets in that I wouldn't change anything. I couldn't. But I am sorry for how I can't…do this with you."

His conviction and sincerity were so deep, they were written in the very lines of his body: the calmness of his breathing, the steady gaze, the loose hands at his sides.

Clearly his freedom was important to him, she thought. And considering the way she felt about being out on the ocean, she could respect that. Yet, why couldn't—

Stop it, she said to herself. Stop trying to negotiate. He is what he is.

"Spike, after this weekend, will I ever see you again? And not in the relationship sense. I know that's not in the cards. I'm talking as…friends?" God, she hated that word.

His chest expanded as he took a deep breath. Before he could speak, she got up and started for the house.

"Actually, don't answer that. I already know what you're going to say."

As Mad got ready for dinner in her bedroom, she kept waiting for Spike to knock on the door and tell her he was taking off.

When the rapping sound finally came, she thought, *okay*…so this was it.

She grabbed the loose black skirt she was going to wear, pulled it on and braced herself as she went to open the door.

The bracing turned out to be a good idea, though not for the reason she'd expected.

Amelia was standing in the hall. "May I come in, Madeline?"

Mad was so surprised, she stepped back and let the woman pass.

Man, check out that dress, she thought absently.

Amelia was wearing an ice-blue sheath and plenty of aquamarines, looking as if she'd stepped out of the pages of *Women's Wear Daily*. As she glanced around, her blond hair shimmered. Positively shimmered.

"This is different from when you stayed here," she said.

"I know."

"It doesn't suit you." The comment was soft, almost an

afterthought, the kind of subtle taunt that had always been Amelia's stock in trade.

Mad straightened her spine. "Thank you for pointing that out. But you didn't come here to talk drapes, did you?"

Amelia's eyes drifted over. "The dark red suited you. It was vivid. Strong. This is too weak to be your room."

Mad frowned. And the expression stuck as a long silence followed.

"Amelia…what are you doing here?"

The woman's manicured hands traced over the pale blue stones at her throat. On another person, Mad would have thought the gesture was a show of nerves, but not with Amelia. You had to care what people thought to be nervous and Amelia had never given a damn.

"How have you been?" the woman asked.

Good Lord, Mad thought. Probably the first time her half sister had ever asked her that question.

"Ah…I'm the same." She shook her head as she realized that wasn't true. "No, I mean, I'm well."

More silence.

"And you?" Mad asked.

Amelia smiled vacantly. "Very fine, thank you."

Mad was not surprised by the social answer.

Feeling fidgety, she tucked her shirt into her skirt and pushed her feet into the only pair of flats she owned. As she looked down, she had a passing thought that Amelia probably didn't have any shoes like this, and if she did, they were not five years old and scuffed.

Mad glanced up. Amelia was staring out of the windows at the garden, completely still. The sight of her absorbed by some distant point was eerie. She was always a whirling dervish of activity, a constant social barometer taking a read on everything around her, assessing, measuring herself, moving on as soon as her conclusion had been reached: always a consumer of the world, though somehow not a participant in life.

Now, though, she looked unplugged, her drive not in neutral, but extinguished.

Okay, enough with the psychobabble. This visit was something from the twilight zone and Mad was beginning to seriously freak out.

"We're going to be late for dinner," she said. "You know how Richard is."

"Yes. Yes, I do." Those gray eyes shifted over. "Madeline, I—"

"You ready to go downstairs?" Spike's voice came through the open door before he did.

He stopped short as soon as he got into the room.

Mad flushed. "Hi… Ah, yes. I am."

Spike glanced at Amelia. "Evening."

From out in the hall, the grandfather clock started to strike. Amelia stared at Mad for a moment and then said, "I'll see you both downstairs."

Mad watched the woman go and was glad when she left.

"Mad?" Spike asked.

She looked at him. Tonight he had on a black silk shirt and dress slacks. With his jagged hair and his thick silver earring and the tattoos on either side of his neck, he looked dangerously male. Stunningly attractive. She eyed his heavy shoulders and remembered hanging on to them.

"Mad?"

She shook herself. "I'm ready to go."

Over dinner, Spike decided that the Maguire family was a freaking train wreck of dysfunction. Which just proved you could live in the most beautiful house on the planet and your life could still be a mess.

Man, if it weren't for the five other couples in the room, the air would have been so oppressive the stuff would have qualified as a solid. Mad hadn't said more than two words and had barely touched her food. Amelia, who was on Spike's right, looked like she was going to splinter apart. And meanwhile Richard sat at the head of the table, all simmering satisfaction as he manipulated the conversation.

Spike had a feeling that if he'd run the scene back about twenty years, this was exactly the way things had been during Mad's younger years: father figure enjoying his top of the food chain status while everyone else was carefully kept off balance. Richard's act was obviously a mixture of nature and nurture.

And all this for what? The money in those supermarkets around the Northeast? It seemed ironic that an investment in bringing sustenance to millions of people had contributed to such an emotional famine in this household.

He glanced at Mad then shifted his eyes to his water glass.

All afternoon, he'd thought about leaving. He'd even packed up his clothes. Clearly, things were worse for Mad because he was here, not better. And the awful part was that he was finding it harder and harder not to complicate her situation even more. He'd almost told her about himself when they'd been in the garden. Had been so close. But laying down the details of his past seemed unfair. Like she needed to deal with that crap on top of the compost heap she was already having to shovel herself out from under?

As he shifted in his chair, Amelia said quietly, "You hate this, don't you?"

He glanced at his plate. "Well, the trout could have been better."

She smiled a little. "I'm talking about the party, not the protein."

"Yeah, well, I'm not exactly a tie-and-cuff kind of guy. So formal's not my bag."

"And yet Richard said you're a French chef." Her tone was friendly, that smile of hers soft. "Cooking in that manner is very formal."

"You ever seen a restaurant kitchen in action? Trust me, even *La Nuit* became a pit during the dinner service crush."

The woman's head snapped toward him. "*La Nuit?* You were a chef there?"

"Yup. My partner, Nate Walker, and I both were."

"When?"

"For me, up until about a year ago." He frowned, then rubbed his jaw, considering Amelia's face. "You know, I thought you looked familiar. You used to go there, didn't you? With Stefan Reichter's crowd."

"Not often." She looked away and played with her trout.

"Man, Stefan was wild, wasn't he? I never expected him to settle down."

Her head yanked back in his direction. "Excuse me?"

"Stefan just got married. Like a week ago. I understand Estella's pregnant, although the word is he wanted to be her husband anyway." As Amelia went white as the damask tablecloth, Spike said, "Hey, are you okay?"

"Oh, yes." She quickly had some wine. Then a little more. "I'm just fine."

"You sure?"

She nodded. After a moment, her coloring came back

and she cleared her throat. "So tell me… You really do like Mad, don't you?"

He shrugged, not about to discuss that kind of thing. "What's not to like?"

Amelia put down her wineglass. "Be good to her, will you?"

As the woman seemed to honestly mean what she said, he took the comment at face value. "As much as I can be."

Which wasn't all that good, was it? The secret he kept from Mad turned him into some kind of imposter, didn't it. And he was leaving tomorrow without looking back, wasn't he?

Well, he was leaving at any rate. He couldn't imagine he wouldn't look back. This thing with Mad was going to linger… Oh, God, it was all over tomorrow, wasn't it? The weekend would be over.

"I'm sorry?" Amelia looked at him with brows raised. "What?"

"I thought you just said something."

"Oh…yeah. No. Nothing at all."

When the table broke up after dessert, Mad was among the first to leave and he was right behind her. Out in the foyer, he took her arm and dropped his head to her ear.

"Let's go for a ride." He was suddenly desperate for the freedom of the night and her on his bike. Because he didn't know if he'd ever have her on his Harley again.

As her spine stiffened, he braced himself for a no.

But then she said, "All right."

They disappeared out of the house and were on the road moments later. He had no idea where he was taking them and didn't care. His past and his present were colliding and he was trapped in the middle, suspended between bad outcomes: one completed over a decade ago, one impending with tomorrow's dawn.

All he could think about was that tonight was his last night with her.

He took them miles and miles away from Greenwich, the Harley eating up the asphalt. Some forty-five minutes later, he realized they were deep in rural Connecticut and that, after a series of random turns onto smaller and smaller roads, he'd probably gotten them lost.

He slowed down and pulled over onto the gravel shoulder, figuring it was time to re-group. The deserted two laner they were on was out in the middle of nowhere: no cars or houses around, only maples and oaks and a small pond. The moonlight was the closest thing to a street lamp they had.

As he engaged the kickstand, she dismounted from the bike and flipped the helmet off. Her hair was tangled at the ends and her skirt wrinkled where she had balled it between her legs to straddle the Harley. She looked a little wild.

Which matched his mood. He felt unhinged and starved. Needy. Clingy. Things that he didn't usually throw out at the world, much less at women.

Mad put the helmet down next to the bike and strolled across the road. He tracked the sway of her walk and the slender curves of her body like she was an animal.

No, that was wrong. *He* was the animal. He'd brought her here, to this nowhere place, to this nothing-counts-because-it's-not-real slice of rural anonymity, for one reason and one reason only. He wanted to take her. Wanted to be covered with her body. And he wanted to do it in the kind of privacy they couldn't find at her family's house, no matter how many doors and locks they had.

He wondered if she knew and hoped she didn't. Because he wasn't real impressed with himself at the moment.

"We should go back," he said roughly. "I've taken us too far away."

She pivoted around in the middle of the road. "Have you?"

"Yeah. Definitely." He bent down and picked up the helmet. "Put this back on. Let's go."

"I don't want to." She turned to the pond again. "I can breathe out here."

Funny, he couldn't. Especially as she reached her arms over her head and stretched. As her body arched in the moonlight, he saw her naked.

Spike put his hand up to his chin and cracked his neck, trying to loosen the tension in his body. Then he put the helmet over his hips and rearranged his arousal with a grimace.

"Let's go, Mad. If you want to stay out, I'll take you the long way home." Yeah, the really long way as he only had a vague idea how to get them back to Greenwich.

"Not yet." She walked down to the edge of the pond, a breeze teasing her skirt around. It was a long time before she turned and looked at him.

Separated by the gray, moonlit road, they stared at each other.

"Mad?"

"Yes?"

"Can you come here?" he said in a deep growl. "Can you come over to me….please?"

She drifted across the road, as quiet and graceful as a ghost. While she approached, he kicked his leg out and around, turning himself toward her on the Harley's deep seat. When she was within range, he reached for her, his hands going to her hips. Through the warm night air, his questioned her with his eyes.

She touched his face. "You look hungry."

"I am." His voice was low, hoarse. "And I feel like I should apologize for it."

"Don't." She put her mouth on his. "I'm hungry, too."

With those quiet words, it was as if she'd popped the lid off of him. His arms shot around her and he spread his legs wide so he could get her into his hips. He was almost out of time and she was everything hot and good and sustaining in the world.

He tried not to be rough, but he pushed up her shirt so he could get at her skin, and gyrated his hips against her thighs, dying to get into her. When she gasped, he eased up immediately, but she didn't pull away. She wrapped her arms around his neck and held on harder.

His hands traveled downward so he could gather her skirt in his hands, but then he stopped.

"Come up on me." He shifted, mounting the bike again. When he reached for her, she went with him, straddling the seat, straddling his hips. "Yeah…just like that. Oh…yeah."

He captured her face in his hands and pulled her mouth to him. The sensations of her weight on him, her warmth, her body, shot his need so high he started to shake.

With a quick move, he slipped his hands down to her shoulders and eased her back so she was braced between the handlebars. The thin silk of her blouse offered no true barrier and neither did the simple, lovely bra she had on. Baring her breasts to the moonlit night, he fell upon her with his lips and heard her cry out.

Maybe he should have slowed down, but she was right there with him, hands tangled in his hair, breath shooting out of her mouth, body arched up against his lips and tongue. He was all screaming instinct at this point, and before he knew what he was doing, he'd wrenched her skirt up around her hips.

As he gripped her panties at the hip, she laughed a little awkwardly. "Spike?"

He nuzzled the side of her neck, thinking how beautiful she was sprawled out all over his Harley. "No one's around."

She looked up and down the road.

He eased back. "I'm sorry…I don't mean to push. I'll stop."

"You're not pushing." She glanced around again. Then smiled. "Do…what it was you were going to do."

He kissed her hard then ripped her panties apart on one side and moved them out of the way. When he touched her, he was utterly transfixed.

Without thinking, he dismounted the bike and fell to his knees in front of her, sliding his palms up the insides of her legs. She became restless as he moved up on her so before he leaned down to her body, he looked into her face.

Her eyes were cracked wide open and he was reminded they hadn't done this the night before. And they were out in the open even if it was the middle of nowhere.

"Is this okay?" he asked, massaging her legs gently.

"Ah….yes. If you…um, if you want to—"

"I do. Until I'm shaking from it. I wanted to last night… Was dying to." He flexed his hands into the sleek muscles of her thighs. "Let me make you feel good, Mad."

When she nodded, he smiled and dropped his head.

Mad could not believe that she was making love at the side of the road on a motorcycle.

But then Spike's mouth found her and she didn't think about anything other than him. As she fell back against the handlebars, the things bit into her shoulders and she lost her balance, but she didn't care. And somehow Spike managed to steady her with his big hands without losing a beat. As he did wicked things to her body, her eyes opened to the vast sky and the stars above—the pleasure he gave her seemed just as magical and endless and incomprehensible.

After a mighty release had ripped through her body and she was worn out from the exertion of the ecstasy, when at last he lifted up from her, she knew there would never be another like him. Their connection was ancient and animalistic. Simple, not complex.

As he got to his feet, it was obvious he was painfully aroused, yet he pulled her skirt down and smiled as if he were grateful.

"Think you can hold on to me for the trip home?" he said with more than a hint of male pride.

"Yes." She braced her arm on one of the handlebars, her head spinning as she eased off the bike. "But we need to stay here a little longer."

When she reached for his belt buckle, he jerked. "Mad, we don't have to—"

"Get up on this bike again. But first…" She undid his pants and pushed them all the way down. "Step out of these."

His laugh was abrupt and surprisingly nervous.

"Feels vulnerable, doesn't it," she murmured with a smile. "Even though we're all alone."

"Yes…it does. But I'm game."

She watched him lose his slacks, loving the play of moonlight over the strength and power and masculine beauty of his lower body.

When he mounted the bike, she eased up on him without hesitation and Spike groaned and shuddered as their bodies came together. So did she.

Their position meant she had to take control so she linked her arms around his neck and used his heavy shoulders for leverage. As she moved, he talked roughly in her ear, saying incredibly erotic things while his hands traveled all over her hips and her back and her legs. Everything faded away as the current flowing between them went from a buzzing hum to a burning roar.

"Wait, Mad," he said breathlessly. "I'm going to… Mad, I'm about to…"

She was too far gone to stop, too lost in where they were joined, in the feel of him, in the giddy sense that she was the one driving them into the wall they were about to slam against.

"Mad, I need to pull out— Oh…Mad."

The inferno overtook both of them at the same time. As she cried out, he let loose with a guttural shout in her ear, going rigid underneath her and then spasming and jerking. Her own waves took her away and she grabbed on to him, frightened of the intensity. He was the only solid thing in the world and she must have been the same to him because he was desperately holding her in his hard arms.

They stayed locked together for the longest time, his hands smoothing gently up and down her back. Dizzy, disconnected from everything but him, she burrowed into his neck, rubbing her face in the short hair at his nape. The air between their bodies was a heady perfume, mingling with the summer night.

I love you, she thought.

And even though it was stupid, she wanted to tell him

anyway. Probably because after what they'd just done, she was comfortable being reckless.

"Spike," she whispered.

"What?" His voice was husky.

"I—"

From over Spike's shoulder, she saw a pair of headlights come over the hill.

"Oh, my God!" She leaped off him and yanked her blouse into place, her skirt fluttering down where it needed to be. She grabbed for his pants, but the car was already slowing down, lights trained on her.

She looked behind her, expecting to see Spike half-naked and cupping his manhood. Instead there was nothing but the bike. Where had he—

The sedan pulled up and its driver's side window went down. An older gentleman smiled at her with concern.

"Miss? Are you okay?"

The white-haired woman beside him in the car leaned around. "Do you need a ride somewhere, dear?"

Mad shook her head and tried to look unruffled. "Oh, no. I'm fine. Thank you, though."

The man didn't seem convinced. "That's an awfully big bike for a woman to handle by herself."

Mad glanced at the Harley. "Yes...ah..."

She brought her arms up and linked them across her chest.

The woman in the car laughed softly. "Come on, Jim. Let's leave her."

The man looked over at who was undoubtedly his wife. "That's not right—"

"She's not alone, Jim."

Mad glanced down...and realized a pair of very long, very man-size slacks were still attached to her hand.

She wasn't sure whether Jim blushed more or she did. And the gentleman cleared his throat awkwardly, though his wife was looking amused in a nostalgic way.

"Evenin', then," the husband said.

"Thanks for stopping," Mad replied. After they took off, she hissed, "Spike? Where are you?"

Spike popped out from behind a massive oak and planted his hands on his hips. He chuckled wryly.

"If any of this green stuff is poison ivy, I'm in deep trouble."

Chapter Eleven

The following morning, the first thing that went through Spike's mind was that he wanted to make it work with Mad. Or at least give it a shot.

It was crazy to let this thing with her go. No way he was going to find anyone else like her so she was worth taking the chance of coming forward again.

She was the one for him. And he was head over heels.

Man, the night before, when he'd watched her walk down to her own bedroom by herself, he'd had to fight to keep from following her. And it wasn't about sex. He wanted to sleep next to her. Wake up with her. Loll around in bed as the sun rose, talking about nothing with her.

Maybe if he told her about his past, she could accept it, accept him. And as for her sailing schedule, he was willing to wait for her on land while she did her thing. The distance would kill him... but it wasn't like he could see himself with anyone else.

Spike rubbed the back of his neck, anxious as hell now that he'd decided to try to talk with her. How would she take what he'd done? If he explained what had happened, would she see him as a monster? He didn't know how he would handle that.

And when should he spring it on her? Maybe he should wait until it was time to go and ask her to spend a couple of days with him. They could get away, go some place quiet like a B&B. He could hold her and talk to her and then they could—

He thought about what they'd done on his Harley and broke out in a hot sweat. Yeah, maybe they could do some more of that, too.

Time for a shower. Definitely.

Ten minutes later, he was about to get dressed when he heard a knock. Cinching the towel around his waist a little tighter, and hoping like hell it was Mad, he opened the door.

Amelia was on the other side dressed in a white satin robe. "I'm sorry to bother you, but may I talk to you for a moment?"

He frowned. "Give me a minute to get dressed."

The second the words left him he thought, Why had she come at the crack of dawn? Something wasn't right. "Actually, now's not a good time."

"It won't take long."

He was about to say no when the woman's eyes got to him. They were dark with raw pain. Regret. Sadness. In fact, she looked as if she were going to burst into tears.

He stepped back and she came in. Mindful of what Mad had said about the woman, Spike left the door open and grabbed for his button-down shirt. Last thing he needed was Mad's half sister all over him.

"What's this about?" he asked, pulling the shirt on and crossing the two halves over his chest.

Amelia's words were rushed, as if she'd practiced them. Maybe for quite a while. "I've made some terrible mistakes. Done things I need to apologize for. Things that were cruel."

"To Mad."

"Yes, to Madeline. And to others. Last night, I went to her room before dinner to apologize. Although even if you hadn't interrupted us, I doubt she would have heard me out."

"Look, if you've come here because you want me to help you with her—"

"I have."

"I can't do that. Mad's a grown-up. So are you."

Amelia looked out a window, avoiding his stare, blinking a lot. "Of course, you're right. It's just…have you ever wished you could take something back? Take…things back. Undo actions?"

Running theme of his life, Spike thought, that constant reassessment of the past. At least for him, he kept coming to the same conclusion, that what he'd done was heinous but…justified by the need to protect someone who couldn't defend herself against a larger, deadly opponent.

Amelia clearly had no such perspective on her acts.

"It hasn't been—" Her voice cracked. "It hasn't been until recently that I've realized how much one person can make another hurt."

When he didn't reply, she dropped her head, the defeat in her totally at odds with her incredible beauty. "I'm sorry I bothered you."

"It's never too late," he said, wanting to ease her because her misery was so complete.

Amelia looked over at him, her gray eyes shining with tears. "Sometimes…sometimes it is. And it appears I've learned *that* too late."

Wait a minute, Spike thought. That expression. That look…something about it triggered his memory. Yes, from his days at *La Nuit*…Stefan Reichter…*Amelia*.

Holy…Moses.

Stefan Reichter had always been a high-flying, great-looking, trust fund junkie; a bachelor catch if there ever was one. The gossips had maintained he'd loved only one woman, a secret woman whom he'd had a long dramatic love affair with before meeting this new, pregnant wife of his. Evidently, the secret lover had spent a couple of years giving the jet-setting playboy a run for his money—and had made him miserable by winning.

The woman's identity had never been known because evidently she'd told him she wouldn't see him in public because he was too Euro-trashy for her tastes. According to city whispers, Stefan had broken it off with this phantom about a year ago because he couldn't take it anymore.

"Good Lord," Spike said. "You were Stephan's…"

And that's why Spike had thought he'd seen Amelia before. It had been at *La Nuit* right before he'd left. She'd looked as crushed as she did now…and she'd been sitting at a table with Stefan and Estella.

Amelia started to leave, as if she wished she hadn't come, as if she feared what he was remembering. As she passed him in the doorway, he shook his head.

"You were the one, weren't you. Stefan's secret lover who broke his heart." Amelia stumbled at the name and Spike caught her with his hand. "You're the one."

* * *

Mad slipped out of her bedroom door and padded down the hall. It was ridiculous to feel like she was sneaking around when she was an adult, but that's what it seemed like.

During the long night hours, she'd despaired that she and Spike weren't laying together. They had so little time left and it was passing quickly. And that was why she needed to be with him now, before the day got rolling, before the shareholders arrived, before…she had to say goodbye to him when there were eyes around.

Keeping as quiet as possible, she jogged down the corridor and went around the corner—

She skidded to a halt. Amelia was standing in Spike's doorway wearing a silk robe. Spike was gripping the woman's arm urgently…while wearing just a towel and an open shirt. He looked as if he were trying to pull her back inside.

Mad's first response was that there must be some kind of explanation. Spike wouldn't do that to her. He wouldn't—

"You're the one," he said.

Mad recoiled as if she'd been sucker-punched.

Ducking back out of sight, she clamped her hands over her mouth to keep from screaming…or maybe it was to catch herself when she threw up.

Wheeling around blindly, she took off, making no noise in her bare feet as she raced back to her room.

When she got there, instinct took over where pain rendered her numb and stupid. She yanked on a pair of jeans, pushed her feet into her Nikes, and shoved the few things she'd brought with her for the weekend into her bag. She didn't bother to change shirts, and flashed out of her bedroom with her duffel while wearing the tank top she'd slept in.

She was down the stairs and crossing the foyer at a race/walk when Richard's voice cut through the nightmare.

"Where are you going?"

She didn't acknowledge him, didn't stop, just punched through the front door and made a beeline for her Viper.

As she tossed her bag into the passenger seat, Richard grabbed her elbow. "What the hell is going on?"

"I'm leaving." She ripped her arm free and got in the car, jabbing the key into the ignition.

He kept her from shutting the door by gripping the top of the thing. "Why?"

She glanced up at him and his little smile told her he suspected the reason. Hell, he'd probably invited Amelia up for the weekend for the sole purpose of enticing Spike.

Mad pegged her half brother with hard eyes, utterly unafraid of him for the first time in her life. "You know exactly why."

"Amelia?" he drawled.

Mad cursed, realizing she'd been played beautifully. By all of them. Spike included.

"You know something, Richard? I should never have come here and I'm never coming back." She yanked the door out of his hold and slammed it then pushed her foot into the clutch. But before she threw the gearshift into first, she put the window down. "Oh, by the way. Do yourself a favor and don't raise any objections about my trust."

"Why must you be so unreasonable—"

"Did I mention I've hired a lawyer? Mick Rhodes. Ever heard of him?" As Richard's mouth closed up tight, she smiled grimly. "Ah, I see you have. Good. Those shares are mine and I'm going to vote them. Back the hell away or get run over. It's your choice."

"Madeline, wait—"

"Not a chance."

"But what about Spike?"

"He's fine. Amelia's taking care of him."

Mad hit the gas and popped the clutch, spraying pebbles all over Richard's linen pants.

Richard watched the Viper take off and realized he might have miscalculated his style of play.

He'd never seen Madeline like that. Ever. She'd been enraged to the core yet deadly calm.

It made him respect her a little.

And while the dust over the drive settled, he churned the implications of what she'd said. Mick Rhodes wasn't a lawyer. He was a paving machine. The guy had leveled more opponents than any other attorney on Wall Street.

How the hell had Madeline gotten access to a man like him? Rhodes's clients were Fortune Fifty companies…but maybe she'd gotten an in through one of her big-money sailing contacts? There were plenty of hard-core corporate players who liked boats—and say what you would about Madeline as a woman, she was, evidently, one hell of a sailor.

Richard crossed his arms over his chest and shook his head. Damn it, with Rhodes on board, the fight to hold on to those shares of hers was going to be a nasty one.

Except maybe all wasn't lost. Clearly, Amelia had worked her magic on that chef, bless her heart. And Madeline was furious right now, riding a wave of anger, talking a good game. But later, when the fury bled out of her, she would know only rejection and hurt and she would revert to her normal state, forgetting about the shares and the trust. Without Spike in her ear prodding her toward independence so he could get his hands on her money, she would let everything return to where it had been.

Richard glanced back at his house, then refocused on the driveway.

The key of course, was making sure Spike stayed away from her. That man might have been momentarily blinded by an attraction for Amelia, but he wasn't stupid. If he were looking for cash, Mad was a much better ATM candidate. Amelia needed money because she spent it constantly and a woman like that, with expenses of her own, would be a much harder target for bilking. Spike was going to figure this out quickly and then he'd go back to working on Mad.

And she was just enough of a sap to let him back in the door. So the mission critical would be cutting that avenue off.

Fortunately, Michael "Spike" Moriarty, had a hell of a history as it turned out. And Richard knew all the gory details thanks to the phone call that had come in late last night from his lawyer. The report on Moriarty's background had been thorough...and thoroughly illuminating.

Surely there was a way to use it to his advantage.

Richard thought about the way Spike and Madeline had behaved around each other and suspected they couldn't have spent a lot of time together. And regardless of her maintaining they were just friends, it was obvious they were having sex; any idiot could have read that over the breakfast table yesterday morning. Clearly, though, it was early in the relationship. Very early. They were cautious with each other still, batting that *friends* word around and ducking glances. To the guy's credit, Spike was playing the cautious suitor brilliantly...while he was no doubt counting the ways he could finance his restaurant ambitions with Madeline's trust.

It was a great thing that Amelia had come between them

already. But there needed to be another wedge in there so Spike didn't think he could come back.

"Where did Madeline go? Did she leave?"

Richard turned around to Amelia and had to smile. "Of course she did. And I have to give you credit, you work fast."

"Excuse me?"

"Please, don't be coy. It's boring. I must say, Moriarty's a bit of a roughneck for you, but I imagine a little change is good."

"You think I... *She* thinks I was with Spike? Oh, God, Richard—"

"Weren't you?"

"No!"

Well...that was a surprise, on a lot of levels. "The tattoos kill it for you?"

"Mad is with him!"

"Hasn't bothered you before, has it?" he said offhandedly.

Richard started to worry but then told himself everything was still okay. Even if the deed hadn't been done, the effect was the same. Madeline would be hard-pressed to get over the perception, however it had come about, that Amelia had been with yet another man of hers. However, the fact that nothing had happened made it even more imperative to convince Spike there was no shot at redemption.

Abruptly, a look of purpose came into Amelia's eyes and that was the last thing Richard needed.

"Drop it, sister. It doesn't matter."

"It does. I must go...and explain. Though I don't know how. And why does she think... Oh, perhaps I do know how she got that impression."

"Don't bother apologizing. She won't believe anything you say because you have absolutely no credibility when it comes to things like this." Amelia took a deep breath and seemed to deflate before his eyes. Which was perfect. "Darling, just forget about it. The two of them never would have lasted anyway."

Without a sound, the butler came up behind Amelia. "Excuse me, the phone is for you. A Mr. Stefan Reichter. He said he's returning your call from last night?"

Amelia blanched. "I....I'll take it in my room. Thank you."

As his sister and the butler left, Richard stared at the front of the mansion. While he thought about Spike and Madeline and trusts and money, he noted absently that the boxwood on the right seemed a little thin.

That bush needed to be ripped out and replaced.

Following that thought, he settled on an idea. It wasn't perfect. It wasn't his best. And it was risky. But it was the only thing he had. And sometimes, as in chess, you had to play the moves you were given even if they were not as strong as you wished they were.

Spike was tucking a black T-shirt into his jeans when the door opened behind him without a knock.

Richard entered and shut the two of them in the room together. As Spike's warning instincts went off, he kept cool.

"I'm going to have to ask you to leave," Richard said.

Spike casually slipped his feet into his boots. "Why?"

"Because you were a guest of Madeline's and she's no longer on the premises."

Spike narrowed his eyes, trusting the man about as much as a three-dollar bill. With a hole in the middle. "When did she go?"

"Just now." Richard went over to one of the windows and pulled back the heavy drapery. "See for yourself. The

Viper's gone. And before you ask why, I'll explain. You see, I told her about you."

"What do you mean you told her about me?"

Richard's eyes were steady. Rock steady. "Your prison record, Michael Moriarty. The five and a half years you did for beating a man to death. His name was Robert Conrad. You killed him by—"

"Why the hell would you tell Mad all that?"

"You need to ask? Don't you know how her mother died? Or was that why you never said anything?"

With a horrible sense of bars locking him in, Spike asked, "What the hell are you talking about?"

"Violent felons sometimes kill innocent bystanders. You didn't happen to, you just took out the one man, but not all murderers have your discretion. Madeline's mother wasn't so lucky when she was killed." As Spike recoiled, Richard went on. "Did you know that Madeline was four at the time her mother died? Old enough to have memories. Old enough to remember how it felt to be told her mother was dead. And to hate and fear the kind of violent man who took her away."

Spike shut down completely. If Mad's mother had died in the course of a felony, of course she would flee. Especially because it looked like he'd hidden the facts from her.

Richard smiled a little. "Ah, yes. So you can see why she wouldn't want to be around you. Especially because you didn't tell her yourself. The association was too painful, but the lying by omission…not very heroic of you, was it? And there's no way to apologize for all that. Not now that it came out as it did. She never wants to see you again."

Spike felt like he was in a nightmare. God damn it, Sean should have told him about Mad's mother. Why had the guy sent him down here to help her when he knew the horrible parallels?

"Spike? I mean, Michael?" Richard stepped in front of him. "I'd like to offer you a deal here."

Spike trained his eyes on the other man. "Deal?"

"I'll fund your new restaurant with Nate Walker provided you stay away from Madeline. I mean, you can understand why I have to protect my sister from you, given your past. But I'm also a businessman and there's no reason to get totally wrapped up in emotions. Just keep away from her and I'll take care of you."

Spike reacted without thinking. He met Richard chest to chest and forced him up against the wall. Then he dropped his head so their noses were almost touching. As he did, he could practically smell the fear that rolling off the other man.

Spike bared his teeth. "You are going to get the hell out of this room right now. And I am going to pack up and leave. That way, no one goes to the emergency room with broken bones. You understand me?"

Richard's voice was high. "I'm just trying to help."

"I doubt that. Now get out of my sight."

The man was out the door in a split second.

While Spike got his stuff together, his hands were shaking so badly, he dropped his wallet. As he picked it up off the floor, he thought of that first night when he'd come in and realized someone had been through his stuff. Richard. Of course. The guy had no doubt taken Spike's social security number and address and run them through the usual databases.

Then the bastard had gone to Mad.

Spike left the room with his duffel, jogged downstairs

and went out to the Harley. It took no time at all to store his clothes in the saddlebags and mount up. When he put his helmet on, he cursed because as he pulled it down over his head, he smelled Mad's shampoo.

Oh…God, how she had to feel knowing what he'd done. The similarities with what had happened to her mother were no doubt nauseating, but the secret he'd kept made the situation untenable. He should never have been with her, never have made love to her.

And she was never going to let him explain. The omission cut her too deep and why wouldn't it.

Spike fired up the Harley and tooled on out. As he headed back toward the Adirondacks, he was aware that he was cracking wide open on the inside. The fact that he had hurt her was…the worse part of the torture.

As soon as he got back home, he was going to call Sean and find out what the hell the guy had been thinking.

Although that was incidental. The true fault was Spike's own. Completely.

Chapter Twelve

"*God damn it!*"

Six weeks later, Spike burned his wrist so badly he went momentarily blind. With a lurch he tossed the saucepan away and dimly heard it clatter across the industrial stove as he went right for the sink. Cranking on the cold water, he shoved his forearm under the spray and kept right on cursing. He was so loud that the sounds of the White Caps kitchen drowned only some of the words out.

Nate Walker looked over from the grill he was manning, flames roaring in front of him. "How bad is it?"

Spike took his wrist out from the water. "Ah, hell…it's blistering up good."

A third-degree burn. And all because he hadn't been paying attention and had splashed hot oil on himself. Idiot. Stupid idiot.

But that was the way things had been going for the last

month and a half. Ever since he'd come back to Saranac Lake on Memorial Day, he'd been a mess, all stuck in his head, making careless mistakes. Hell, he'd nearly sliced off his pinkie the day before.

With a grunt, Spike cut off his curses because he figured no one else needed the air show. Reaching for the burn cream they kept over the sink, he buttered up his wrist and wrapped the thing with gauze. Then he headed back over to the stove.

"Oh, no, you don't," Nate barked. "You need to get that looked at *now*. Reynolds, take over for Spike on sauté. Frankie! I need hands on salad."

Tom Reynolds, the line cook, turned away from the small plates of leaves he was working on and went for the stove. Meanwhile, Nate's wife, Frankie, put down the napkins she was folding and went over to the salad station.

"Two filets for pickup!" Nate called out as he tossed another sirloin on the grill. A mighty hiss was released as the steak landed. "Moriarty, you hit the road right now."

Spike shucked his white apron and headed for the door, feeling pretty damn replaceable. When he remembered he'd come on the Harley, he turned to ask Nate if he could borrow the guy's truck. With the pain as it was now, operating that bike was more than he could handle.

His partner was already tossing the keys to his F-150 across the kitchen. "Doc John will see you as a walk-in. Just knock on the back door. And don't bring my wheels back until tomorrow."

When Spike went out to the truck, he was about as mean as a snake.

And as he took the Lake Road into town, his mood only got worse. There was a lot of summer traffic, but it was of the lovey-dovey pedestrian variety. Couples strolled at the side of the road, holding hands or walking arm-in-arm while they looked out at Saranac Lake. It was the same when he got to the town square. Couples. Always couples. Since when had the world become full of people in love and looking at each other with doe eyes?

It was enough to make a guy sick.

Doc John's office was just off the town square and housed in the old Victorian ark the guy lived in. Spike went to the back door as ordered and Saranac Lake's only physician got up from a meal with his family to take a look at the burn.

As they walked down the hall to the clinic, Doc John said, "So, I guess you did yourself a good one if you're coming to see me. Usually you cook types wait until something is falling off before you'll show up here."

"It was a stupid mistake."

"They usually are."

The two of them went into one of the treatment rooms. With Doc John's brawny build and beard, the guy looked more like a woodsman than a physician, but somehow, this just made Spike trust the man more.

While the doctor washed his hands and snapped on gloves, Spike hopped up onto the exam table.

Doc John came over and reached out to remove the gauze. "So how's business at White Caps? I've heard busy."

"Yup— *Good God*," Spike hissed as the man started to unwrap the burn. Just the act of taking off the dressing was enough to make a guy put cracks in his molars.

"I'll go slower," Doc John said.

"No, just do your thing. I deserve it for being such a jerk around the stove."

When the doctor got a gander at the wrist, he shook his head. "I wish you hadn't put that salve all over the burn. It's not what I want on there right now and I'm going to have to clean it off."

"Do whatever, Doc."

"I'll be right back."

A couple minutes later, Spike's whole forearm was in some kind of solution and the two of them were staring at it, watching it soak.

"Doc, can I ask you something?"

The guy reached out and pushed Spike's hand down so it, too, was covered by the liquid. "Anything."

"If a woman…" Spike cleared his throat. "If a woman doesn't get her period, does that mean she can't get pregnant?"

"Nope."

The anxiety that had plagued Spike for the last month and a half sat up and howled. "But what if she isn't ovulating?"

"How does she know she's not?"

"Because she's an athlete and her body fat is so low—"

Doc John shook his head and pushed Spike's hand back under again. "No, I mean, how can she be sure? The human body has a way of doing what it wants. There's only one sure way to prevent pregnancy and that's abstinence."

Spike felt the blood drain out of his head. He'd known this, damn it. He'd known all of this. He should never have—

Doc John glanced up and offered a smile. "I don't mean to personalize this, but you might ask her to take a test if you two are worried."

"She was really sure it was okay." God, he sounded lame.

Yeah, but as he thought about the situation, there was something even worse. He realized he would love to have made her pregnant. And how appallingly desperate did that make him?

Doc John shrugged. "You mentioned she's an athlete with low body fat? Then that increases the likelihood that she isn't ovulating, especially if she's not getting a period. But nature can find a way. Go buy a test at the supermarket. Put your mind at ease."

This was said as if he and Mad were a couple. Who lived close to or maybe even with each other. Who were there to support one another.

He felt like throwing up he missed her so badly.

Except then Doc John poked at his wrist and he just plain felt like throwing up.

When Spike left a half hour later, his forearm hurt so badly he could barely see straight. The physical stuff, though, was a minor inconvenience compared to the tortures his head was going through. He drove home in a daze, knowing that he'd be no good to anyone in the kitchen at White Caps and not just because he couldn't lift a sauté pan to save his life.

The apartment he'd been living in since he'd come to Saranac Lake was on the top floor of yet another one of the town's Victorians. He had two bedrooms and a kitchen and a living room and he liked the place. There were windows in every room and the floors were hardwood and it was a quiet building.

As he drove up to the house, he saw that lights were on at the top and he was glad. His nomadic sister, Jaynie, had been staying with him for the last couple weeks, and tonight, he'd just as soon not be alone.

He parked around back, parallel to the picket fence, but then just sat there in the truck. A compulsion he'd been trying to fight since Memorial Day got too hard to battle any longer. He shifted his hips and dug his cell phone out of his jeans pocket.

After he was finished talking to Sean, Spike hung up and did some more staring.

The night after he'd left the Maguire mansion, he'd called Sean, wanting to know why the guy hadn't thought to mention the stuff about Mad's mom. But Sean had been out of the country in Japan still, and by the time the man had returned only days ago, it seemed unnecessary to rehash all the ins and outs of the disaster.

No, tonight, Spike had wanted to know only one thing and Sean had told him.

His buddy hadn't seemed too surprised by the question, either.

Eventually, Spike got out of the truck and used the rear stairs. When he opened the back door and walked into the kitchen, he heard the sound of typing. Immediately, it was cut off.

"Spike—"

"It's just me—"

He and his sister spoke at exactly the same time. She never had gotten comfortable with being alone and he was always careful to shout out as he came into any place he knew she was in. Especially if she was by herself.

"You're home early," she called out from the front of the apartment.

"Yeah." He shut the door and went to the fridge. Orange juice would be good right now. Cold. Sweet.

As he poured himself a glass, his sister came into the kitchen. "What— Oh…are you okay?"

"I'm fine." He glanced over his shoulder.

Jaynie was standing in the archway, a slight woman in her very early thirties, wearing shorts and a T-shirt that were at least two sizes too big for her. She also had a sweatshirt across her shoulders, even though they had no air-conditioning and it was hot. With her dark hair pulled back and her wire-rimmed glasses, she reminded him of a sparrow, quick and brown, hypervigilant.

"Spike, what happened to you?"

"Nothing a few days off won't cure." He swallowed the orange juice under his sister's stare. "Jaynie, I'm okay. It's just a little burn. How's the work going?"

She held his eyes for a moment. Then seemed to accept the fact that he wasn't going to talk about what he'd done to himself.

"Well…I'm slow at it. Medical transcription is like holding water in your hands. Words keep slipping through no matter how fast you go. But it's better than some of the things I've done and the pay is okay." She pushed her glasses farther up on her nose. "You know, I wish you'd let me give you something for the rent."

"And I wish you'd try and stay here for more than a month or two. Hell, move in permanently. I told you, I really like the company."

He also *really* liked knowing she had a roof over her head and a place where she could sleep safely at night. Well…not that she slept much at all. He'd heard her walking around a lot after hours.

"So how about not being a guest anymore," he said. "How about becoming my roommate?"

"We'll see."

Which meant no. But at least she was here now.

He stared down into his glass. "Listen, Jaynie, I need to

take a little trip tomorrow. Just an overnight. Will you be okay here on your own? Nate and Frankie are a minute and a half away. In fact, you could stay with them—"

"I'll be fine. This is a safe building."

"I won't be gone long."

"Is this about Madeline?"

Spike's head whipped up. "How did you—"

"You say her name. In your sleep." Jaynie flushed. "I'm not eavesdropping. It's just, when I'm up, I hear it. You sound like you miss her."

He exhaled. "I, ah…yeah, this is about her."

His sister's soft smile transformed her face, making her utterly beautiful. "Good. It's about time you cared about someone enough to miss them."

The following afternoon, Mad stood on the deck of a seventy-five-foot sailing yacht and watched the land on the horizon grow larger. Newport, Rhode Island, was nothing but a smudge on the top of the sea right now, just a strip of dirt that looked like you could wipe it off with a paper towel. Soon, though, it would be three dimensional and over-whelming, trading places with the ocean for supremacy.

She'd spent the past month and a half putting the rehabbed America's Cup boat through its paces and doing over-nighters on other yachts down in the Bahamas. Then she and two of the crew had hopped on this boat and made the Newport run with a pair of sailing hopefuls who wanted a shot at the big-time. The trip had been successful. Both newbies had proven they had good sea legs and fast reflexes. Plus they could handle themselves with Bonz and Jaws, two of the toughest sailors around.

"Mad Dog, what is *up* with you?" Bonz sidled over to her,

all blond hair and tanned muscles. His real name was Garrison Fitzhugh Bonnycastle IV, but he was Bonz to everyone in the sailing world. "You've been so damned quiet."

"Nothing doing." As he rolled his eyes, she said, "Hey, do you know when Hoss's boat is going out for the Caymans?"

"Tomorrow morning first light. Me and Jaws were going to crew but we need some downtime."

"Wonder if there's still a berth available."

"For you? Hell, Hoss would pitch his own mother over the gunwale to get you on one of his boats."

"You say the sweetest things."

"Truth, not charm."

For a little while, they were silent, both focused on the sea. Then Bonz's hand landed on her shoulder.

"Time for a caring and sharing moment here, Mad Dog."

"Oh, no—"

"So listen up and I'll get through it quick. Jaws is worried about you, too. And if you don't tell me what's wrong, I'm going to be forced to let all the boys know you're upset about something."

"There's nothing—"

"Think about it. All twelve of us. All over you. Until you tell us why you've been so quiet since Mem Day."

She smiled and glared at him at the same time. "You are bullying me."

"Without hesitation or remorse."

She had to chuckle. "Well, I appreciate your concern… I think. But it's nothing."

"Come on, Mad Dog. What's under your skin? Spill it."

"Fine. You win." She grabbed the front of her shirt and swooned, throwing one hand over her forehead. "I've got a broken heart."

Bonz barked a laugh. "Yeah, right. Over a man? I'll believe it when I see it. You'd be more likely to get upset over a bad day in the wind. Why can't you be honest? I mean, I figure you'd be psyched on life right now. Crew's in good shape. Boat's fine. Our buoy times have been great."

"And so am I. Great, just great."

He stared at her and rubbed his jaw. "I'm getting nowhere here, am I?"

"Nope." Even though she'd actually given him the truth. Spike was a curse, a man who had betrayed her who she couldn't get out of her mind. Her heart was utterly broken. "I'm just fine."

Bonz leaned in close. "You're lying."

As he walked off, she thought that was certainly correct. The six weeks away had done nothing to make her feel better and the idea of being trapped on land for even a day made her want to scream.

Alone on deck, she watched Newport get bigger with dread.

Two hours later, at around six in the evening, they were docked and unloading gear at the New England Yacht Club. The N.E.Y.C. was a superexclusive enclave of ocean-faring folks and it looked the part, all pristine white buildings, perfectly maintained boat berths and landscaped lawns. There were at least fifteen world class sailboats anchored off its quarter mile of shoreline and there were more yachts tied within its maze of docks.

Hoss's eighty-five footer, her escape hatch, was just four boats over from her. Pausing, she assessed the *La Belle Femme* with approval. The trip to the Caymans would be a long one. A good one. And Hoss probably would boot off anyone he had just to get her on board as navigator.

But before she went to find him, she had to finish her work here.

While storm clouds gathered, she humped gear and unused supplies off the boat with the men. She figured when they were done she'd find Hoss, then go into town, check into a hotel and collapse. She was utterly exhausted from sailing for forty-five days straight and she figured she was tired enough to actually pass out. Which was just fine with her. Maybe she wouldn't have to deal with the nightmares she'd been suffering through lately.

As she lifted a pair of five-gallon water jugs out of the hold and up on deck, she was very aware that her force of will was keeping her going, not her muscles. Yet when Bonz took the dead weight onto the dock, she just went back for more.

In the distance, she heard a dim thunder and wondered whether the storm was gearing up already. When the sound rolled to an end, she didn't think any more of it, just kept reaching for the next bag and the next box and the next jug. Until she realized there wasn't anything left.

Mad glanced around the hold. With everything out, the cleaning crew could come in next and scrub down.

"That's it," she called up to the deck. Thank God.

"You want to meet us in the bar?" Bonz yelled down to her.

"Yeah, in a minute."

"Good. And listen, stop by the front desk. When I went to register us, they said they had a package for you."

As the men took off, their low voices faded and she closed her eyes for a moment. Then she went fore to the six berths that were stacked one on top of the other in pairs. She and the men had slept in rotating shifts. Bonz snored. Jaws talked in his sleep. The other two had been dead quiet either because they were totally pooped or unable to sleep at all.

Her duffel was sitting on her bunk and she fished around in it until she found her new cell phone. With slow fingers she dialed in to the separate number she'd given folks to call when she was at sea and found that there were nine messages.

Which was a surprise even though she hadn't checked the thing for at least a week.

Two messages were from Sean and they were the kind friends left when they were worried, but didn't want to press. One was from Alex Moorehouse asking her about her schedule. Then there were five from Richard, none of which she listened to. The final one was from Mick Rhodes, who'd tried to reach her on the cell and failed. Fortunately, it was good news.

As she hit #2 over and over again to clean the mailbox out, she thought of everything Mick had done for her. He was the reason she'd gotten the cell phone and the only one who had the number. Over the past month and a half, he'd called her down in the Bahamas a number of times, updating her on the situation with her trust.

Right after Memorial Day weekend, Richard had brought an action in court to block his being unseated as executor of her trust. And Mick had taken care of her half brother swiftly and decisively. She didn't know exactly what had transpired, but clearly it had been hardball. Within no time Richard had retracted the lawsuit and she was free of him.

She supposed she should have felt triumphant. Instead, she was resolved.

Mad zipped up the duffel and slung it over her shoulder.

As she headed out, she figured finding Hoss wouldn't be tough. He'd either be sitting in the club's bar watching the storm come in with the boys or he'd be at his house on Millionaire's Row. If she didn't catch him here at the club, she'd walk down Bellevue Avenue to his place after dinner—

She stopped at the foot of the little stairwell to the deck.

What was she thinking? She couldn't go on that damn trip with Hoss. She had to be in Manhattan for the Value Shop Supermarkets board meeting the day after tomorrow.

Good heavens…how bizarre to have something on her radar screen other than sailing.

Mad emerged out on deck and took a last, long look at the ocean. The storm was churning, coming on fast, darkening the sky. The clouds were so heavy with rain, they were purple as plums.

When she turned around, Spike was standing on the dock.

Her first and only thought was that it was cruel of him to look so good. Black leathers and biker boots. Jacket hanging from one of his hands. Black hair standing up straight off his head. Golden eyes like the sun.

It was as it had been the night he had arrived in Greenwich: a total shock. A lightning flash of attraction. An instant quickening in the air.

The time away from him had changed nothing. He was still captivating. But then she remembered other things about him.

Anger lit off in her chest.

Spike was prepared for the worst, and as he waited for Mad to step back with fear or contempt or disgust in her eyes, he absorbed the sight of her, sucking in every nuance. She was tanned and looked healthy, except for the bags under her eyes. And good Lord, she was lovely. Her hair was French braided but the wind had freed some strands and blown them across her cheeks. He wanted to put both his hands on her face, sweep the dark pieces back and… kiss her hello.

Which was so not going to happen.

"What are you doing here?" she asked in a tight voice.

"I came to see you."

There was a long pause. "How did you get into the club?"

Her utter lack of reaction chilled him to the bone. "I used to work the grill here in the summer. Everyone knows me."

"Naturally." She leaped off the boat in a graceful move and walked right by him. "If you'll excuse me, I was just leaving."

"Are you pregnant?" It wasn't at all what he'd wanted to lead with. But she was taking off fast, and if nothing else, he had to know.

She froze, then looked over her shoulder. Her eyes were narrow. "No, I'm not."

"Are you sure?"

"Yes."

"How do you know?"

"Because I do."

"Did you take a test?" God, this was not going well. He'd wanted to try and reach her, try to explain…something, anything. Instead, they were locked into this clinical conversation that was making him sick to his stomach and clearly pissing her off.

"I'll call you if there's a problem, okay?"

"A child with you wouldn't be a problem for me," he whispered.

As her eyes popped wide, he realized he'd spoken the thought out loud.

"Well, it would be for me," she snapped.

Spike had to look down at the dock. He'd been slapped a number of times in his life. Punched much more frequently. Stabbed twice, too. But nothing in his memory could touch the pain that was barreling through his body right now.

"Yes, I could imagine it would be," he replied quietly.

There was a long silence. When he finally looked up, she was staring at him with an odd expression.

"At least you seem to regret what happened in Greenwich," she said.

"Of course I do." He would rather have told her about the past himself. Maybe her reaction would have been different.

But then he thought about the way her mother had died. Ah, hell. Probably not.

"I have to go," she said.

He wanted to make her stay. Didn't have any right to. "I'm so…very sorry."

Her eyes went to the sea and he was willing to bet she wished she had stayed out there. "Me, too."

"Will you let me know if—"

"Yes, I will." Against the darkening skies, her profile was a stark, pale contrast, like a cameo pin. "But I'm not pregnant."

"You don't know how to find me. Let me give you my number—"

"Sean will have it, right? So I'll talk to him if I need to reach you."

With that, she turned away.

Spike watched her walk off, her duffel bag brushing against her hip and her braid swinging from side to side. Her strides were even, her footsteps sure. She did not look back.

For some strange reason, his vision was suddenly eclipsed by memories of the moment when his whole life had changed over a decade ago. He remembered pounding up the stairs to a grungy apartment, saw himself throwing open the door, and then...the horror of his sister on the floor, curled into a ball, arms protecting her head. Above her, a six-foot-two man with a baseball bat lifted high.

Spike shuddered and refocused on Mad.

She was entering the clubhouse now, and as the door shut behind her, he realized his life had changed yet again. One door opening, twelve years ago in that run-down apartment; one door closing at this very moment, in a ritzy private club.

Neither event was significant on the surface; doors were used every day, passed through every day.

Some, though, some turned you into something else...or in this case, kept you right where you were. On some very basic level, Spike realized his future was going to be nothing more than decades of his present: A lonely stretch, made lonelier now because he'd had a glimpse of what *together* might have been like.

After a long while, he went around the clubhouse, walked out to the parking lot and got on his Harley.

Doing the whole ride back to the Adirondacks would be tough this late, but he could get a head start. Or maybe he would just drive through the night. His arm was aching, but he didn't care. Nothing could reach him right now. Nothing.

And his numbness gave him a strange, troubling kind of invincibility.

As he started Bette, the first raindrop fell.

Mad's knees were loose as nylon ropes as she walked into the clubhouse. After she picked up her package from the front desk, she went upstairs to the ladies' lounge. The large airy space was done in the club colors of red and white and it usually cheered her. But not now.

When she dropped her duffel from her shoulder, she didn't hear it hit the floor, but she was careful with the FedEx box, setting it down right next to her bag. Taking a deep breath, she went over to the bank of sinks and washed her face. With water dripping off her chin, she grabbed a white towel with the N.E.Y.C. insignia on it and draped it over her entire head.

Six weeks...six weeks she'd spent thinking about Spike and running through that morning at the Greenwich house over and over again, seeing him reach out for Amelia, hearing him say, *You're the one.*

Mad was desperate for some way she might have mis-construed the situation and this was dangerous, like reading the wind when you were out at sea racing and badly behind. The peril in looking too hard was that you would invari-ably convince yourself that what you wanted to find was out there. When it really wasn't.

She thought of Spike in all that leather just now. He'd said he only wore the supple armor if he was traveling long distances. So obviously he'd come all the way down to Rhode Island to see her. Why had he—

He'd wanted to find out whether she was pregnant. That was the why.

And she truly wasn't. She'd wondered about the same thing and had taken a test right before she'd left the Bahamas. It had been hell to do, so hard for her that her hands shook the whole time. But the really sick part of those minutes when she'd stood over the sink, checking her watch and looking at the stick, was that part of her wanted to be. Which was flat-out insane. She couldn't possibly handle being a single mother, which was what she would be; Spike being in her life was not healthy for her—not that he'd offered anyway.

And then it was all a moot point. The test had been negative.

As Mad glanced down at herself, she saw that her hand was on her lower belly and the yearning in the gesture was tragic, frustrating.

Great. Terrific. Her biological clock was still kicking in.

Except it wasn't really hormones, was it? No, it was the image of a little baby with black hair and yellow eyes, and how lousy was that? It was utterly self-destructive to want to carry the child of a man who had played her.

A crack of lightning lanced through the sky and the boom that followed was sonic. As rain started to fall, she looked at her watch. Driving to Manhattan didn't appeal, not in a storm, not this late. It was far better for her to find a B&B in town and leave first thing in the morning.

Mad shouldered the duffel again, picked up the FedEx box and left the lounge. She knew what was inside the overnight delivery: the materials for the board meeting. Going by how heavy the thing was, she knew there was a lot, but she had every intention of going through each page until she'd memorized what was on it. She might not have a background in big business, but Mick Rhodes had said she could call him anytime with questions and she was sure Sean would be willing to help, too.

Mad left the clubhouse, not feeling up to dealing with the boys in the bar, and jogged out through the downpour to the garages beyond the parking lot. While she'd been away, the Viper had been housed in one of the rentable car stalls, and the engine fired up so fast, it was like the thing wanted out.

Crouching over the wheel, she headed into town, wipers slapping madly yet losing the battle against the deluge. Thunder crashed above her, all around her.

The tears came slowly at first. But by the time she pulled around to the back of the Lancet Bed and Breakfast, she was weeping openly.

As she sobbed, she realized why she was having a meltdown here and now. This moment in her car was the first time she'd been alone since she reunited with the crew.

While the storm raged, she let herself go and cried until she had nothing left.

Chapter Thirteen

Spike was soaked to the bone by the time he walked through the front door of the Lancet B and B. He'd gone over the bridge to Rhode Island proper, made it maybe five minutes in the storm and realized he was crazy. He turned and went back to Newport because he knew for sure where he could find a place to stay.

The Lancet House was an historic landmark, a rambler of an old mansion with ten guest rooms and a nice kitchen. Needless to say, the B and B was a huge step up from where he'd slept when he'd cooked summers at the New England Yacht Club—back in the day, he'd crashed on couches, assuming he'd slept at all.

The room he was given for tonight was small, but it was dry and luxurious. He peeled off his leathers, stripped the rest of himself bare and hit the shower. Ten minutes later he was down in the house's dining room, sampling a buffet dinner with the other guests.

As he sat down and tucked into some roast beef, he felt a kind of isolation no crowd could cure. In fact, he was so removed from everyone, he felt as if he were watching a movie about people eating their dinners and talking to each other. In black and white.

Except suddenly some kind of ripple went through his body. He looked up.

From across the way, through doorways and archways, around the moving bodies of other guests, he saw Mad come in the front door. Her hair was damp, water was dripping off her duffel bag and she looked wretched. As she checked in, she seemed unaware of her surroundings, and when she went up the stairs, it was as if in a total daze.

Heart in his throat, Spike waited and waited for her to come down, until all the other guests in the dining room had finished eating and had drifted out to whatever their evenings held.

As a rolling growl of thunder permeated the mansion, it was clear the arrival of another storm was imminent.

He looked out the window to his left and sipped his cold coffee.

He was willing to bet Mad hadn't eaten anything at the club.

But that was none of his business, he reminded himself.

"Are you finished with the buffet?" a waiter asked. "Because we'd like to put it away now."

Spike glanced up at the guy. "Ah…yeah. I'm finished with it."

Mad eased back against the pillows and stretched her legs out. It was always disorienting to lie on an unmoving bed after having bunked it on the ocean for a couple of days. But man, it was good. And the superhot shower she'd taken had also done wonders. It was a guilty pleasure to just stand under the spray until her fingers pruned up and her feet turned bright pink.

Now, lying down in a terry-cloth robe marked with the Lancet's insignia, she felt a little stronger, provided she didn't think too much about the accommodations. Her room was lovely. Romantic. Perfect for a weekend spent indoors. With its antique four-poster bed and its marble fireplace, she imagined many couples had found or rekindled passion here.

Not wanting to think about that kind of thing, she dragged the FedEx box onto her lap and ripped it open. Inside were three spiral-bound books of financial statements, memoranda and graphs.

She opened the book marked 1 of 3, figuring she might as well start at the top and hoping there was some logic to the order. The first page was an agenda and she skimmed the issues. Approval of the minutes of the previous meeting. Election of officers. Financial report for the fourth quarter. Summary of performance for the prior fiscal year. Acquisition of Organi-Foods Corporation.

Whoa. She knew that name. Those stores were everywhere.

She flipped through the books until she got to the tab marked Acquisition Proposal. When she was finished reading the memo from Richard to the board, everything about his fight to keep her shares fell into place. If he retained voting rights over her block of ownership, he could push through stuff like this acquisition with no problem because, in effect, he was the majority shareholder times a thousand.

No wonder he'd wanted to remain executor of her trust. Now, he'd have to convince her to get anything done.

That must have been what all the phone calls from him were about.

She heard a knock at the door and lifted her head. "Yes?"

"I brought you dinner."

The muffled sound of Spike's voice had her sitting up with a jerk.

"I can leave it out here in the hall," he said quietly. "If you'd feel more comfortable that way."

She sprang off the bed, straightened the robe she had on and opened the door.

"I don't want—" But she couldn't quite finish the sentence. He was so broad, filling the jambs, his black T-shirt stretched over that chest she knew too well.

Damn it... The distraction of his body disgusted her. Didn't she have willpower? Common sense?

And what had happened to his forearm? There was a big white bandage all the way around it.

Not her concern, she told herself. And neither was the rest of him.

She kicked up her chin. "I didn't know you were staying here."

"Or you would have gone somewhere else, right?" When she didn't reply, annoyance flickered over his face, tightening his mouth. "Do you honestly think I'm a threat to you? Just because I'm across the hall?"

She frowned, thinking that was a weird choice of words. "Of course not."

Well, not a physical one anyway.

"Good," he muttered. "So prove it. Invite me in and eat what I brought you."

"I'm not—"

"Hungry? Oh, right, I forgot, you're Super Woman. Capable of going for days on nothing but air." As she opened her mouth to tell him off, he cursed and dropped his glowing eyes. "I'm sorry…I take that back. Look, here's the food if you want it."

He held the plate out to her and for some reason she took it. "Thank you," she said. And then hesitated.

"Invite me in, Mad," he said softly. "Please. I'm not looking for sex or anything like that. I just want to explain some things. I want to tell you what happened and why."

Do not let him in, she thought. Do not—

God help her, she backed away from the door and left it open. He shut the thing silently as he came forward.

She sat on the bed, put the plate in her lap and unrolled the napkin full of silverware. He was right, she wouldn't have eaten and she wasn't sure she wanted to now. Her stomach was in a knot, but she needed to do something with her hands.

While she tried some of the roast beef, she tracked him as he went over to one of the windows across the room. In the silence, she despised the fact that she was hoping and praying he would come up with an excuse she could buy.

Frustrated with herself, she said, "You don't have to explain why you were with her. I know the why of it."

His head spun around and a frown dragged his brows down over his eyes. "What?"

"Why you slept with Amelia. I know why. It's obvious why."

Spike reached out for the window, grabbing on to the sash as if steadying himself. "You think I… Where in the hell did you get the idea I was with her?"

"Come on, Spike—"

"Why do you think I would do that to you?"

His intensity was a surprise. "I— Ah, I saw her walking out of your bedroom and you were trying to pull her back in. You were very clear you wanted her."

Those yellow eyes stared at her for a long stretch. "Hold up. You left because—"

"Oh, no, I really wanted to stick around after that. Absolutely."

Her sarcasm didn't seem to affect him at all. "Wait… Richard didn't talk to you about me?"

"Why would he have to? Seeing you with my half sister was enough."

Spike scrubbed his face with the palm of his hand. He seemed to have shocked out for some reason, his eyes going glassy. "Good…God."

"Come on, Spike," she muttered. "Do you think I'd hang around? I've been through that twice before. The experience has nothing left to teach me."

Which was not exactly true. This time it had hurt worse than the others put together.

Spike was silent for a moment, then he threw up his hands and shook his head. "I…I don't know what to say. I guess…enjoy the dinner, Mad. And…whatever. Take care of yourself."

He walked to the door like every bone in his body hurt…and as if he were giving something up.

What the hell was wrong with him? She was the one who'd been betrayed.

"Why do you think I could handle it?" she said as he gripped the doorknob. "Knowing that after everything we…did together, you went to her?"

"Yeah, that would be awful," he snapped. "Just about as bad as your total lack of faith in me."

She put the plate aside and got to her feet. "I just *cannot* believe this. Why are you so ticked off?"

He wheeled around and faced her. "You don't think it would be just *slightly* offensive to be accused of sleeping with your half sister?"

"But you did, didn't you? So why—"

"No. I. Did. *Not*." His eyes were blazing. "I have no idea what you saw—"

"The two of you were in the doorway to your bedroom and you were half naked! She was in a robe!" Mad dropped her voice and tried to stop her body from trembling. "Do you honestly expect me to believe you didn't want her—"

"She's nothing like you," he hissed.

"I realize that. And you told *her* she was the one."

Spike opened his mouth. Then shut it so hard his teeth clapped together.

Mad pushed her hair out of her way and dug her hands into the robe's pockets so he wouldn't notice how badly they were shaking.

"Look—" she cleared her throat "—I... Boy, there's really nothing more to say, is there?"

He stared at her for a long time. When he finally spoke, his voice was eerie. Flat. Deflated. "You are very right about that."

And then he left quietly.

After the door shut, Mad told herself he had a hell of nerve acting like the one who'd been injured.

She fumed for a while, then went back to the bed and looked at the plate he'd brought her. She had no interest in food.

But she cursed and picked up the damn fork, remembering the vow she'd made to herself: No more running on caffeine. No more not eating, no matter how much weight she put on. She had promised herself the moment she'd landed in the Bahamas that she would stop the excessive dieting and let her body get back to normal.

So Mad ate because it was the right thing to do, not because the stuff tasted like anything. And as she chewed and swallowed like a robot, she thought about the argument just now with Spike.

He'd looked so...defeated as he'd left. And why had he asked if Richard had spoken to her about him? Why would that matter?

And why had he said he hadn't slept with Amelia?

Spike had never struck her as a liar, but was he just a really good con man? Or was there something totally off about this whole situation?

Mad tried to go back to reading the board meeting materials, but couldn't concentrate. She felt as though she were on a boat in high seas: tossed, turned, thrown around. And the real-life storm outside didn't help. All the lightning and thunder just kept the frantic pace of her heart going.

Not long thereafter, she gave up. She just couldn't shake that defeated expression on Spike's face. And though she was worried about her sanity, she shifted off the bed and went out into the hall to the guest room across from hers. The door was ajar and she heard running water.

"Spike?"

"You just missed him if you mean Mr. Moriarty." The woman from the front desk poked her head out of the bathroom with a smile. "He's left."

Mad's rib cage tightened up. "I... Ah, where did Spike, I mean Michael, go?"

"Said he had to head back home." The woman shrugged. "Was very nice about it. I was going to give him some of his money back but he wouldn't take it."

A gust of wind pushed up against the house and rattled the shutters. Then a rush of rain hit the windows in a splatter pattern, hard as buck shot.

Oh, God. Spike on that Harley. Going back to the Adirondacks in the dark. In the storm.

The woman reached behind herself and cut the water off. "Say, I noticed you missed the buffet. Would you like me to bring you up something?"

"Thank you, but...no. Someone already has."

Mad returned to her room. Closed the door. Climbed back up on the bed.

She told herself it was good that he'd left. She wanted him so badly she was liable to get seduced into thinking what she'd seen with her own two eyes wasn't true. Hell, maybe the seduction had already happened.... Maybe he was just a really convincing actor and that's why she was so conflicted now. Because after all, how well did she really know him?

Mad rubbed her eyes until they burned and thought of the other two times she'd been in this nightmare. Both of the other men Amelia had taken from her had come back with apologies—after they'd been summarily dumped. So the fact that Spike had returned and tried to explain himself followed the pattern.

She'd done this all before.

Without warning, a bolt of lightning flashed right outside the B and B, bright as a bomb detonation. The cracking sound of a tree trunk being split was instantaneous and she jumped, clutching the lapels of the robe to her throat.

Damn it, were these storms going to last forever?

A half hour later, Mad was pacing. And not just because of the argument with Spike. The furious weather was unrelenting, obviously a chain of T-cells linked together, flowing up the coast.

She stopped next to the bed and looked at her cell phone. When she picked the thing up, she dialed Sean's cell number.

"O'Banyon," he said when he answered. In the background she could hear voices as if he were at a party.

"Sean?"

"Mad! Is that you? Hey, you'll never believe who I'm here with."

"Who?"

"Your good buddy, Mick. He and I are out on the town tonight. The two of us decided we needed some time off."

"That's great…" God, now she felt awful for interrupting him.

"You okay, Mad?" Before she could answer, he said, "Here, hold on a minute." There was a rustling sound, then his voice was muffled as if he had his hand over the receiver. There were more noises and then when he came back on, the din had faded. "What's wrong?"

She blew out her breath, wishing a whole lot of things were going better. "Spike was here in Newport after I docked, but I think you already know that. Because you told him I was coming in, didn't you?"

There was a curse, then, "Yeah, I did. He said he positively needed to see you face to face and he asked me to keep quiet because he was afraid you'd bolt if you knew he was coming. I'm sorry, Mad. I felt like hell about it, I really did. But he sounded so—"

"It's okay." And she didn't really fault Sean, especially not with all that regret in his voice. "But can you do me a favor?"

"Anything. My conscience is dying for redemption."

"Can you call Spike and see if he's okay?"

"Did it go that badly between you two?"

Yes. "No, it's because of the storms. Spike left in them."

"Oh, yeah, we're getting hit here in Manhattan, too. Rotten weather tonight. But don't worry, he's a good driver."

"He came on his bike, Sean."

There was a tight silence. "I'm calling that idiot right now."

"Will you let me know if he's okay?"

"Absolutely. That damn fool idiot—"

As the connection cut off, Mad curled her phone up into her hand. And then realized she hadn't given Sean her cell number. But no matter, she thought, it was no doubt logged in his caller ID.

Her phone rang right away and she answered it. Sean's voice was sharp.

"Mad, I'm getting voice mail. I'm going to keep trying until I get through to him. I'll call you as soon as I finish yelling at him to get off the damn road. Unless…you want me to have him call you?"

"No."

Sean's inhale was long; his exhale short and hard. "I had hoped things would work out for you two."

"Thanks. But don't tell him about this phone tree we've got going on, will you?"

"Mad—"

"I mean, all of this is a little high school, I realize. I

just…yeah, I'd rather talk to you." Before he could reply, she said, "Oh, and I guess I have two favors. The board meeting is the day after tomorrow. Do you think I could come stay with you? I was going to drive down to the city as soon as morning comes."

"Sure. I'll be at work, but you have a key. And listen, if you need help with the board materials, I'll come home early."

"That would be great."

"Mad?"

"Yes?"

"Am I honestly forgiven for telling him how to find you?"

"Yes, Sean." She smiled a little as she hung up.

It was awhile before she could get back on the bed and try to go through the board books. And even as she returned to the reading, a big part of her brain was focused on her cell phone. Which didn't ring.

The night wore on and so did the storms. She must have fallen into a hazy half sleep because when her phone finally went off, she jerked awake and scrambled for the thing.

"Sean?" she said.

"He's home safe. He called me back as soon as he got the first of my eight pissed-off messages. He was exhausted, said he was soaking wet and going straight to bed. But he's fine."

Thank God. "I really appreciate you doing this."

"Yeah, well, I'm going to break one of his legs when I see him next, just so you know. Now go back to sleep."

"Good night, Sean."

She hung up and looked at the clock. Two forty-eight in the morning.

He'd ridden all the way back. In the rain. With his forearm in rough shape.

Her instincts vibrated. No man put himself through a trip like that casually.

Something was missing in this picture, she thought, closing the books and turning off the light.

She just didn't know what it was.

An hour or so after he got home, Spike rolled over in sheets that were tangled in his legs. He suspected he was awake, but as he opened his eyes, he wasn't so sure.

He was...lying in a bed that was not his own. Except... wait, he'd been in this bed and in this room before, had seen the lace at the windows and the rose glow of the walls...he just couldn't remember when or why—

Mad's bedroom. Yes, this was where it had happened for them for the first time. Where he had gone to her and kissed her and taken her...

Images of them making love had his naked, aroused body twisting on the bed. He could feel her underneath him, giving way as he pressed inside of her. The rhythm...yes, the rhythm of the sex and the heat of her. She was here now with him and they were moving together, locked at the hips, with him about to—

Except then he was alone.

As he looked around, feeling cheated, Mad came in through a door.

Even though it was dark and she was only a shadow, he knew she was gloriously unclothed and looking at him. When she didn't come closer, he tried to call out her name, but for some reason, he couldn't speak. Desperate to communicate, he used his muscles and bones to talk for him. He arched his back and swiveled his hips, offering himself to her and not just his body, either.

She stepped up to the bed and a light suddenly flared.

She had clothes on now, a whole lot of them. In fact, she was wearing a ski jacket and snow pants.

As he lay naked on the bed, Mad stared down at him as if considering his invitation to have him. Then she shook her head and zipped up the parka even higher on her neck. *I'm sorry*, she said. *You leave me cold.*

Spike bolted upright, not so much waking up as being ejected out of the dream.

He cursed and rubbed his hair.

Well, wasn't that symbolism apt. Her covered in Gore-Tex and goose down. Him naked and aching. Couldn't his subconscious be a little more original?

He groaned as he shifted his legs off the bed and got to his feet, so aroused his whole body felt stiff. Disgusted with himself, he went to the bathroom and splashed cold water in his face until he was calmer. Then he checked the clock. 4:00 a.m.

As he'd fallen into his bed around 2:45 a.m., by all that was reasonable, he should be heading back for more shut-eye. But even after that endless, miserable motorcycle ride through the storms he knew he wasn't getting any more sleep tonight.

The apartment was hot as hell and he needed some air, so he put a pair of boxers on and wandered out of his room, being as quiet as possible. On the way to the little porch in the front, he paused beside Jaynie's partially closed door. Her light was off and for once, it appeared she wasn't awake.

When he'd come home unexpectedly, she'd been surprised to see him, but she hadn't asked questions. For which he'd been grateful.

He left his sister sleeping and went across the living

room. He was about to open the porch's screen door when he stopped. Up on the wall, there was a calendar of dogs, one that Jaynie had hung. July featured a border collie leaping into the air to catch a Frisbee.

When Spike looked at the date, he felt a twisting sense of vertigo.

Two days before the anniversary of him killing Jaynie's abuser.

Good Lord.

Over the last couple of years, he hadn't thought of the past very much. Not the specifics of it, at any rate. But all the stuff with Mad had dusted off the memories and now, with that number on the calendar so close, everything came back even harder.

Man, did he need some air.

Unlatching the screen, he stepped onto the shallow porch. The night smelled of pine and summer warmth, a thick, woodsy aroma that under different circumstances would have eased him.

Not tonight.

And not for a long time, he feared. There would be no easing him for a very long time.

Chapter Fourteen

Two days later, Mad sat in Sean's kitchen, surveying the mess of papers on his glass table. It looked as if a snow cloud had opened up and dumped a load in his breakfast alcove.

Around eleven o'clock last night, she and Sean had ended up dismantling the three board books; it was either that or risk tearing pages from all the flipping back and forth among the sections. And that wasn't the worst of it. A legal-size pad had been used down to its cardboard back, its scattered innards marked with her handwriting and Sean's diagrams.

She was amazed at how far she'd come.

Well…how far she had come in regards to the board meeting.

There had been no progress with the situation involving Spike; she was still a mess on that front. But at least in the midst of that, she'd truly come to understand Value

Shop's business basics. And she knew what was going to happen at the board meeting—especially when it came to Richard's acquisition proposal.

Sean had been incredible. They'd stayed up half the night with him patiently answering her questions and explaining things. When he'd said he was impressed by how quickly she was catching on, she'd been so overwhelmed she'd burst into tears, shocking them both.

She wasn't a candidate for an MBA, not by a long shot. And she wasn't angling for Richard's job or anything like that. But she did feel she had enough of a grasp on the fundamentals to have one very strong, very important opinion about the company's future.

When the doorbell went off, the surprise of the noise brought her back into focus. Stretching, she put down her pen and padded in her bare feet across the penthouse's floors. The marble and hardwood were cool under her feet; the Orientals warm and a little furry.

"Did you forget your key, Sean?" she said as she opened the door. "And weren't we going to meet after the meeting—"

Amelia was standing on the penthouse's threshold, looking like a St. John ad.

"Hello, Madeline," the woman said quietly. "I was hoping you would be here, but I wasn't sure."

Forty-eight hours ago, Mad's response would have been to slam the door. But now all she thought about was that look on Spike's face after their argument at the B and B.

Maybe her half sister showing up was fate. Or maybe Mad was just opening the door to get hurt worse.

Ah, but this was not part of the pattern, was it? Before, the men had come back. Never Amelia.

"Madeline, may I please come in? I've wanted to talk to you since Memorial Day. Actually, before that, too. I had hoped, while we were in Greenwich…" Amelia drifted off into silence awkwardly. "I'm babbling."

Mad felt like she was jumping into the ocean without a life jacket, but she stepped aside and motioned with her arm. It would never have dawned on her to go looking for the woman, but since she was here, it seemed worthwhile to hear her out.

As Amelia came in, so did her perfume. The scent around her was light and lemony, perfect for her navy-blue and white clothes, completing a carefully constructed look. Except it was funny. The clothes and the hair and the makeup and the jewelry all coalesced into a gorgeous statement of wealth and ease, but it was Amelia herself who didn't fit the picture. She looked…worn out. Ground down.

Mad shut the door. "Amelia—"

"The day you left Greenwich, Richard told me it was because you thought I'd been with Spike. I wasn't. I wouldn't do that to you."

Mad opened her mouth to point out that the woman had twice before. But then she changed the direction of her words. "I saw you coming out of his room. Why were you there if you hadn't spent the night?"

"I'd gone to ask him if he would talk to you for me. I've wanted to apologize to you for a while now, but you've always been away. And I thought there was a good chance you wouldn't listen."

This was *definitely* not part of the pattern, Mad thought. Everything was off here. Gone was Amelia's iron-clad confidence, her nose-up disdain, her sharp smile and sharper calculation. In their place? A ruined woman.

With a chill, and because she wasn't sure she could trust anything she was hearing, Mad asked, "What…has happened to you?"

"I miscarried seven months ago."

Mad felt her eyes pop as she brought her hand to her throat. "Amelia…"

"It was unplanned, but that didn't matter to me. It still doesn't. I am…devastated." The woman took a deep breath. "And my lover is married now, his wife pregnant with twins. I never told him about the baby…at least not until the weekend you and I were both in Greenwich. When I finally explained to him what had happened, he didn't believe me. Accused me of creating the story to engender sympathy. Oh, Madeline, I lost the love of my life because of my arrogance and now I suffer alone."

Tears welled in Amelia's eyes and they were not of the crocodile variety. Her face had gone blotchy and a red flush had crept up her neck. She seemed barely able to hold it together.

"My baby would have been born this week." Amelia cleared her throat. "I wanted to tell you these things because if I didn't, you would never believe me when I told you I was sorry for what happened in the past. For what I did to you with those two boyfriends of yours. And you also wouldn't believe me when I told you that whatever you saw in Spike's doorway, he and I were never together. Never. I wouldn't do that to you now and it was clear that morning that he never would have."

Oh, God, Mad thought. Spike… Spike hadn't lied.

Panic and a choking sense of urgency flooded her chest. She had to go see him. Immediately— Oh, hell…the board meeting was in two hours.

Right afterward. She would drive up to Saranac Lake and see him in person right afterward.

Amelia wiped beneath her eyes. Once, twice. "I was so evil. And I'm so very sorry."

Mad refocused on her half sister and her heart stilled as she thought of what Amelia appeared to have been through. But then she had to ask, "What I never understood is why. Why did you do it? I was never any threat to you. I was the ugly tomboy."

Amelia wrapped her slender arms around herself, her Hermès bag falling in front of her hip. "Do you know what Papa told me when I turned eighteen? He told me that I was lucky I was beautiful as the rest of me was unredeemably unattractive. All along, he told me that my looks were the only thing I had to leverage in the world and because I believed him, I used them... I used them for fun and out of desperation and because I was bored. I used them because I actually liked the men or maybe I wanted something. And sometimes...sometimes I used them to hurt people."

Mad measured Amelia, looking at a woman she'd always assumed was unbreakable. Her half sister didn't seem that way now; she looked as though she was going to shatter apart. The difference was so astonishing...the revelations so unexpected, Mad didn't know what to do.

"That's all I came to say." Amelia glanced around the penthouse, then met Mad's eyes. "I understand if we can't have a relationship because of all those years. I can't imagine trusting someone like me would be easy. I just...couldn't live with this hanging over me anymore. I can't fix what happened to my baby or the man I loved. But this, with you... This was something I could do something about."

Amelia walked over to the door. Then she paused. "You

should know that Richard called me and invited me out to Greenwich that weekend. He's never done that in the four years since Father died and I believe he wanted me to come because you were there. You and a man you liked. Be careful of Richard, Mad. He's very smart and he gets what he wants. I don't know why he needs to have you and Spike apart, but for some reason he thinks he does."

As Amelia stepped into the hall, Mad called out, "Wait."

Her half sister glanced over her shoulder.

Mad found it hard to let go of a lifetime of bad memories of the woman. But she was willing to…to do what? It would take time to trust. A lot of time. Did they have enough of that in front of them?

Mad found herself hoping so. But that wasn't why she stopped Amelia. "Are you going to the board meeting this afternoon?"

Her half sister frowned. "I never go to them. Richard votes my shares because I gave him a durable power of attorney. Why?"

"Before you leave, I want you to see something."

Chapter Fifteen

Jaynie Moriarty came into the kitchen through the apartment's back door, put her bags of groceries on the counter and looked out toward the living room.

Yup. Through the little porch's screen door she could see Spike's big shoulders overflowing one of the white plastic chairs. He was out there again. Had been out there for two days straight, staring at the mountains and the lake in the distance and no doubt seeing nothing at all.

Jaynie put the hamburger and the milk away and left the bags of chips and the cereal out on the counter. After pouring two tall glasses of lemonade, she headed for her brother.

Whether he knew it or not, it was time for that man to do some talking.

Nudging open the screen with her hip, she looked at Spike. He was leaning back in the chair, bare feet up on the railing, eyes fixated on nothing in particular. His jeans were old, torn and baggy. And loose, as if he'd lost weight.

"It's hot," she said, putting a frosted glass in front of him.

He jerked, his breath going in sharply. "Oh—yeah. Hey, thanks."

Jaynie sat down in the plastic chair next to him. She'd never seen him so distracted before and knew it wasn't frustration that he couldn't work with that bandaged wrist of his. The poor man hadn't come home soaking wet at two in the morning the night before because things had gone well with that Madeline woman.

And Jaynie wanted to know that had happened, but experience had proven that prying would get her nowhere with her brother. The trick with him was to get a conversation going and let him jump in with his own goods when he felt like it. And he usually took the bait, provided she wasn't direct.

She took a nice long sip of the icy lemonade and said, "I think I'm going to go look for an office job of some kind."

"Transcription stuff not working out?"

"No, it really isn't."

"So you're considering staying here for a little while?"

Yes…as long as she was able. Which wouldn't be more than a year probably. She was always found, no matter where she went.

"Maybe," she replied, "but I need to make more money if I do because I should get a place of my own. I love living with you, but you should have your privacy."

He smiled, but the expression didn't last long. "Got no need for privacy."

"Still—"

"I'd rather you stay with me, how about that?" He frowned. "Are you sure I can't find you something at White Caps—"

"I told you, I don't want favors. But I read in the newspaper that the Algonquin Hotel on Lake George is looking for some seasonal help."

Her brother's eyebrows came crashing down. "That's like forty minutes away."

"The drive isn't bad."

"Jaynie—"

"I might not get the job anyway. But I'm going to try."

He looked at her and seemed to realize she wasn't budging on this. "Well…let me know if I can help anyway."

"I will. And thanks."

There was a long silence. And when he cleared his throat, she knew she was going to hear about what was bothering him.

"It happened today," he said. "Twelve years ago."

Jaynie's whole body went cold. Twelve years ago… that night when Spike had taken the life of her abuser to save hers. Good Lord, usually she remembered. "Yes…today."

Now they were both looking at the view and seeing nothing.

With stark clarity, she recalled the horrifying series of events that had happened so long ago, reliving them in slow motion. And then she remembered the terrible silence afterward…the silence and the way Spike had looked with blood on his hands and horror in his eyes. Later, the ambulance had come for her and Spike had left the scene in handcuffs.

"Do you still think about it?" she asked.

"Not day to day, no. But once a year. Right about this time, yeah, I do." He glanced over at her. "Do you ever talk about it with anyone?"

She shook her head. "For a long time it was because I

was still so emotional. But then it was because I didn't trust people. Now…it's because I don't have anyone. Well, I haven't…had anyone."

She stopped there, not about to tell him the whole story as to why she was alone.

Spike shook his head. "You mean, all this time you haven't dated anyone?"

Oh, this was so not where she wanted to go. There were things he couldn't know. "Not really, no. I just haven't met anyone—"

"Even after all these years—"

"Yeah, okay, you're really making me feel like an old maid here. What about you? Have you spoken about it?"

He stared into his glass and Jaynie noticed absently that the color of his eyes was almost as yellow as the lemonade. "No. There's been no one to talk to for me, either."

The name Madeline seemed to hang in the air between them.

"What about that woman you went to see in Newport?" So much for not prying directly.

Spike took a drink from his glass. "That was a no-go. And man…the ending of it was really whacked. I thought it was because of the prison time I'd done. Turned out she just didn't trust me at all."

"You're completely trustworthy."

"Not in her eyes. And I didn't even go into the past with her. Hell…if she didn't have enough faith in me to begin with, no way she'd have been able handle the ex-con thing." He tilted the lemonade up and swallowed a couple of times, then wiped his mouth with his hand. "Especially because her mom…her mom was an innocent victim in the course of a violent felony. It would take a special kind of connection to work through that kind of thing and we didn't have it. At least not on her side."

"Were you in love with her?"

"Okay," he said briskly. "Back to you and the job search. Are you sure I can't try and get you something in this town?"

Like hell he was changing the subject. "Spike, I'm really sorry. Do you understand that? I hated that you did what you had to do to save me. And that you went to prison… The longest days of my life were when you were suffering for what I volunteered for."

His eyes bored into her. "No woman *volunteers* to get beaten. And no man worth his name allows it to happen, especially if he walks in on it. You did the best you could."

She clamped a hand over her mouth, trying not to cry. "No, I didn't. I should have left him before you—"

"I would do it all over again," Spike said in a dead voice. "The act and the time. To save you, I would do it again."

Jaynie put the glass on the floor between them and buried her face in her arms. Only to feel a solid, soothing palm land on her back.

"It's okay," Spike said softly.

"I ruined your life because I was too weak to get away from him—"

Spike's voice became very quiet. "He would have killed you if you'd tried to leave, you know that, right?"

Oh, God…yes…she'd known that. She hated to think about it, even now. But it was…horribly true.

Eventually, she lifted her head, wiped her eyes and offered him a watery smile. "I still can't forgive myself."

"There's nothing to forgive."

She shook her head but wasn't going to argue. "How is it possible we've never really talked about this before?"

"We haven't been in the same house for long enough. That's why I was so glad when you called and wanted to come up here. That's why I want you to stay."

Jaynie reached out and took his hand. "You know something…that woman who doesn't trust you? She's crazy."

He shook his head. "Madeline's—"

"Absolutely crazy."

Mad was nuts. Certifiable. Completely crazy.

Because she was way too calm.

At quarter of three in the afternoon, she stepped out of a cab and tilted her head back, looking up, way up, into the sky over Manhattan. The Chrysler Building was impressive from any angle, but the view from the ground was overwhelming.

So she really should have been scared.

Instead, she gave her black suit jacket a good yank at the hips, squared her shoulders and marched over to the doors. After she went through the security check point, she got into an elevator with six other people. Everyone was in suits, and she imagined even with her height and her tan, she looked like the others.

She got off on the third floor from the top, stopped in front of a nicely dressed receptionist and was shown into a large conference room with a huge, egg-shape table in the middle. The place was filled with more people in suits and smelled like fresh coffee and aftershave.

Richard was in the corner with Charles Barker.

Mad headed for the first empty seat she saw and put her board books on the glossy table. There was a notable lull in conversation as she sat down, but she ignored it by shuffling through the packet of additional materials that was arranged like a place setting in front of her chair.

For the next fifteen minutes, Richard pressed palms with the other nineteen board members, working his way around the table.

When he got to her, he leaned down. "You never returned my calls."

"What was the point?" she said calmly, looking him right in the eye.

He seemed taken aback and he moved on with a frown.

The meeting was started by Charles Barker and the pace was brisk. Senior staff members made reports, questions were asked, answers were given. She kept quiet. Until the very end.

The subject of the acquisition of Organi-Foods was last on the agenda and Richard stood up to make his presentation. While he talked, it was obvious by Charles Barker's body language that the board's chairman didn't approve: Barker crossed his arms over his chest and stared straight ahead, lips tight.

When Richard and his management team had finished fielding questions about the proposal, Barker cleared his throat and spoke in a flat voice. "I'm asking for a vote on whether to proceed with the proposed acquisition of the Organi-Foods Corporation. All those in favor, say 'aye.'"

Mad was the first to speak up. "Aye. And I have a proxy to vote my sister's shares, as well. They are in the affirmative also."

Richard just about fell out of his chair. And so did Barker. In fact, a ripple of gasps went through the boardroom.

Mad sat back in her chair and met all the stares coming at her calmly. The voting continued, but the decision had been made. By her and Amelia putting their shares behind the merger, it was a done deal.

Various technicalities were discussed and then the

meeting was adjourned. She was out the door the moment Barker rapped the table with the tip of his Montblanc pen.

She'd made it all the way to the elevators by the time Richard rushed up to her and took her elbow.

"Madeline," he said. And then he seemed to stall out. In the background, the post-meeting chatter spilled out of the conference room.

"Yes?"

"Why didn't you oppose me?"

She shifted her board materials around to break his hold on her and punched the down button on the wall. "Because it's not about you. It's about the right thing for the company. Your business assumptions are correct. If we don't expand we can't compete, and with increased volume sales, we can offer better discounts. Barker can't seem to see this for some reason. Which tells me he's probably not the right person to chair the board."

Richard's eyes nearly rolled out of his head as the elevator doors opened.

She got in and turned to face him. "You, Richard, are a nasty piece of work. You always have been. But you happen to have incredible business sense. As CEO of our father's company, you're in the right role. Just bear this in mind. I'm voting Amelia's shares from now on as well as my own. And if I don't think you're the right man for the job, I'm going to fire your ass in a heartbeat. Now, I want an analysis on the prospective, post-merger market opportunities delivered to my post office box in Manhattan the day after tomorrow. Goodbye, Richard."

After the double doors closed, she sagged against the mahogany paneling.

She supposed she should have felt triumph or satisfaction or a rush of power. Instead, she was fixated on one thing and one thing only.

Getting to Spike.

Chapter Sixteen

"What the hell are you doing here?"

As Spike walked into the White Caps's kitchen, he shot his partner a dry look. "Nate, my man, I've got to do something. Can't sit on it any longer."

"You've got a third-degree on your wrist. You've been off forty-eight hours."

"Like I said, I'll roll napkins. But I can't sit at home."

Nate's eyes narrowed, but then he smiled. "Fine. Go into the back room and work that paper. We've got bills to process."

Spike winced. "You are such a bastard."

"And you can still go home."

Spike perpetrated an ungentlemanly gesture, got a kiss blown in return and then went into the office.

Standing in the doorway, he faced off at the piles of bills

and other business-related paper nightmares on the desk. He would almost rather be at home doing nothing. Almost.

Man, this was like choosing between watching paint dry and copying the phone book in longhand.

He went over and sat in the creaky wooden chair, only to stare out the window. The sun was low in the sky, setting over the far mountain range, and down below, Saranac Lake was smooth as glass. The reflection off the water was a molten peach.

He rubbed his chest. He was lonely. He missed Mad—

Damn it, there had to be some way of getting her out of his mind.

Spike looked at the desk. Paperwork. Maybe that would do the ticket. Maybe he could just bore the preoccupation right out of his head.

At ten o'clock that night, Mad stopped the Viper in front of a large Victorian that was just off Saranac Lake's town square. The trip upstate had taken her about four and a half hours. She barely remembered a minute of it.

What a nice house, she thought as she looked at the facade. And so homey, at least from the outside. She would have expected Spike to live in something more modern.

She stepped out and glanced up to a small porch under a cupola at the building's very top. The glow in the window beyond reassured her that even though she didn't see the Harley, maybe he was in.

The front door to the house opened easily and she double-checked the mailboxes. Sean had told her that Spike lived in the uppermost apartment and sure enough, there it was: Moriarty, 3rd floor.

She took the broad stairs all the way up and knocked.

"Who is it?" a female voice said through the door.

Mad frowned. "Oh…I'm sorry. I thought that Spike Moriarty lived here."

Or maybe he did and he wasn't alone. Her heart started to pound. Good God…what if he was with a woman right this very moment?

As she began to panic in earnest, there was a clicking sound while a lock was turned and then the door opened as far as a brass chain would allow. A petite woman with brown hair looked out. Her eyes, behind glasses, were some kind of blue.

"Spike does live here, but he's at work," she said. Then that pale gaze narrowed. "Your name wouldn't happen to be Madeline, would it?"

"Ah…yes, it is."

"Have you come to make nice?"

Mad just about fainted. "I, ah…yes, I've come to apologize. Yes."

The chain was dropped and the door opened all the way. A small hand was extended. "I'm Jaynie. His sister."

Still feeling a little light-headed, Mad shook the palm that was offered, amazed that this slight, quiet woman was Spike's sister. The two had absolutely nothing in common. Not the yellow eyes or the jet-black hair or the size. Not the charisma, either, it would seem.

Mad snapped herself into focus, aware that the woman was waiting for her to speak. "Madeline Maguire. I'm pleased to met you."

Jaynie nodded and they dropped hands. "Listen, he's not going to be home for a while. Where are you staying in town?"

"I'm…not." Boy, she hadn't thought this through, had

she? She'd only been thinking about getting to him, not what would happen after she was finished talking to him. Where the hell was she going to spend the night?

"Do you live not far from here?" Jaynie asked.

"Actually, I drove up from Manhattan. When does he get home?"

"Sometimes not until after midnight."

"Oh. I, ah…I have to talk to him." Maybe she could sleep in the car for a while and come back. It was ten now—

"Would you like to wait for him here?"

Yes, Mad thought. For however long it took. At least she'd be guaranteed a chance to see him this way.

"Thank you. I'd really appreciate that." Mad walked through the door and looked around the apartment. Walls were linen white, moldings were varnished wood, there were windows everywhere. Not a lot of furniture and no pictures or paintings, but the place didn't feel stark somehow.

And then she saw it. Over in the corner, Spike's leather jacket was hanging off the back of a chair and she wanted to hug the thing. Smell it. Get close. God knew the leather was almost as soft as his skin in some places.

Jaynie shut the door, locking and chaining it as if she were in a big city. "I was about to have something to eat. Have you had dinner? I know it's late…"

"Oh, that's kind, but you don't have to feed me, too."

"There's plenty to go around. Honestly. Spike hates to cook at home, so I feed him when he lets me."

"Well…then that would be terrific. I haven't eaten since lunch." Mad followed the woman into a kitchen with a table and two chairs. The smell from the oven was fantastic…onions, spices… "What is that?"

"Just meat loaf." Jaynie took a pan out of the oven. "And I boiled up some corn."

Ten minutes later, the two of them were eating together. And Mad had figured out how Spike and Jaynie were alike. They both had that essential separation from the world, as if there were a glass wall between them and everyone else, one that they looked through, but never walked around. As if they had something they kept to themselves.

"How did you know my name?" Mad asked eventually.

Jaynie cleaved a piece of butter off the stick she'd put on a little saucer. As she ran the pat up and down her ear of sweet corn, she seemed to be carefully considering her words.

"He's missed you. He calls out your name at night."

Mad closed her eyes. The idea that he might have been hurt because of her, made her feel so much worse. "I made a mistake. I made a terrible mistake."

"Yes, you did. I don't know any of the details, but I'll tell you this, my brother is totally trustworthy. And he's willing to do anything for those he loves. Trust me, he gave up years of his life for mine."

"Years?"

Jaynie put her knife down, lifted her corn up, then paused. "My brother has something he may choose to tell you. If he does, try and hear it with an open mind. He deserves at least that from you. He deserves…so much more than he's gotten out of life."

"What is it?" Mad breathed.

"Not for me to say. Just know that he saved my life and not metaphorically. Without him, you and I wouldn't be sitting here enjoying this corn. Butter?"

The woman picked up the saucer and held it out.

In a daze, Mad took some of what was offered. "Thank…you."

Spike didn't leave White Caps until he was thrown out by Nate at midnight.

The office was spotless as he left and at least the paper pushing had passed the hours. He couldn't say he felt much better, but at least the accounts receivable and the accounts payable were both up to date now.

Even though his wrist was aching, he took the long way home on the Harley, going up into the mountains. The country roads were a God send, working their magic, stripping him for a while of everything that was jammed up in his mind. With nothing but himself and Bette's single headlight traversing the twisting paths through the bumps and peaks of the Adirondacks, he found a little calm and treasured it because he knew it wasn't going to last.

When he came back down, he approached his place from the back side, going right into the lot behind the Victorian.

Climbing the rear stairs to his home, he wanted a shower and some shut-eye, but was only confident about getting the first.

The apartment was mostly dark, but he knew the place by heart so he walked through its shadows without a problem. He poked his head into his sister's room. Her bedside lamp was on and Jaynie was asleep with a book wide open next to her. He was tempted to turn her light out, but figured that would only wake her up.

When he got to his room, he shut his door so he didn't disturb her and he didn't bother with lights or lamp switches. He striped naked and went for the shower, giving himself a quick soap up.

He was toweling himself off as he headed for his bed.

And that was when he saw Madeline Maguire was on top of the thing.

He nearly jumped out of his skin.

Then he realized he was naked. He scrambled to cover himself, expecting her to sit up in a rush and say something. Except she was obviously out cold.

He walked a little closer to her.

She was stretched out on top of his navy-blue comforter, wearing some kind of black jacket and pants outfit. Which explained why he hadn't seen her: she blended perfectly into the inky pool of the bed.

Oh…man. He couldn't take a deep enough breath. Was this another dream? He hadn't seen her car…but then he had come home the back way. Had she parked in front of the house?

And if this wasn't a dream, why had she come?

"Mad?" When she didn't move, he reached out and shook her shoulder a little. Her hair was unbound and all over the place, as if she'd been tossing and turning and he wanted to put his hands in it. "Mad, wake up."

She said something softly. And then grabbed on to his hand and pulled him on top of her like a blanket.

Somehow, he managed to keep the towel around his hips as he fell forward. And after he landed on her, he had every intention of getting right back up again…but he didn't stand a chance. She wrapped her arms around him and then her legs and that was it. He sagged against her in spite of his confusion.

"I'm dreaming, aren't I?" she murmured, arching her body.

Her hands found the lip of the towel and then the thing

was just gone. And she was touching him, running her palms up and down his spine.

Spike hissed as he became instantly aroused, but he wasn't about to do anything with the erection. No matter how much—

Oh, *whoa*… Her hands were at his hips now. Then moving underneath them, around to the front—

He tried to jerk out of the way. "Mad," he croaked. "Wake up."

He squeezed his eyes shut and bit his lip hard as she touched him.

"I was so wrong to doubt you," she said, nuzzling into his throat. "And I couldn't get here fast enough to tell you. I'm so sorry… You smell so good." Her lips pressed into the side of his neck. "Mmm…you just washed your hair…"

This was exquisite torture.

He did his best to stop his lower body from flexing and retreating and flexing again, but it found a rhythm, working his arousal within her hand.

Breathlessly, he groaned, "Mad…Mad, wake up."

"Don't want to wake up." Her voice was a mere whisper, the words fuzzy on the edges. "Horrible since Memorial Day. Sad. Missing you. Cried. But now I have you."

She certainly did.

Except the unhappy emotion in her voice calmed the mad lust in him. He lifted his head and brushed her hair back. The torment in her face broke his heart, and even more than her apology, it was what bridged the gap between them. He could deny her nothing when she was so obviously upset. Most especially not himself.

"I don't want you to cry," he said, pressing a kiss to her forehead. "Not over me."

"Only over you. Love you."

Spike stopped breathing all together, unsure he'd heard that right. If he had…

His heart started to pound in his chest. "What was that, Mad?"

"I love you."

Mad came awake just as the words left her mouth.

At first she was totally confused. It seemed that somehow Spike was sprawled on top of her, a glorious, heavy weight, his body smelling like cedar soap and feeling very male…especially where her hands were touching him.

She blushed and let go. "Oh, God…I'm not dreaming, am I?"

As she looked up into his face, she expected to see some kind of anger. Instead, he was staring down at her with tenderness.

"No, you're not," he murmured. "But…maybe I am."

"Did I just…say what I think I did?"

"Yeah." In the dimness, she saw that his eyes were moving around her face. "Do you mean it?"

"Yes," she said without hesitation. At this point, she figured she had nothing to hide, nothing to lose. "Look, Spike, I came here to tell you that—"

He cut her off with his mouth, kissing her deeply, his tongue a powerful surge between her lips. But then he rolled off and reached for something over the side of the bed. As he arched back and stretched his arm out, she saw every line of his body…including that incredible arousal.

Oh…good…heavens.…

He dragged the edge of the comforter over and covered himself. "Mad, we need to talk."

She rubbed her eyes. "I know. That's why I came. I'm so sorry I didn't believe you about Amelia. I really am… I talked to her about the whole thing, but I should have had faith in you without that."

"It really killed me that you didn't trust me."

"I know—"

"Because it meant I couldn't tell you something about myself. Something that is probably going to change your opinion of me. I figured if you didn't have enough faith that I wouldn't do something absurd like sleep with Amelia, you and I would never be able to deal with my past. So we'd never have…you know, a future."

What was this, she thought, a strange hope sizzling across every inch of her skin. She'd come to apologize and do the right thing. But she'd never dreamed…

"A future?" she murmured. "Spike…I thought you don't do relationships."

"Me, too. But you're different." His eyes traveled over her. "You've been different since the moment I first saw you coming out of that bathroom at Alex's. Then when I went out to Greenwich, I tried to do the right thing and stay away from you, but I failed. By the end of Memorial Day weekend, I'd thought maybe we could have something…but then you left and I assumed it was because Richard told you about me."

"He didn't say a word." Joy started to gather speed, but then anxiety gathered in her chest instead, tightening her ribs. "Spike…what don't I know about you?"

His deep breath made her nerves go off until they were a wild jangle. "Mad…I went to prison. For a long time. Years."

She wrapped her arms around herself. "What for?"

"I killed a man."

"Dear…God." She closed her eyes, hoping, praying it wasn't in cold blood. "Why?"

"To save Jaynie's life."

Mad looked at him, thinking about what his sister had said at the dinner table. "Spike…there was no choice, was there? She was in…mortal danger, wasn't she."

His eyes darkened from conflicted feelings. "There was no other way. I had to do it."

"But then why did you go to prison?"

"You can only raise self-defense against a murder charge if you were the one being attacked. I wasn't the one he was going after with a baseball bat." As she flinched, he said quickly, "I'm sorry. I don't want you to feel…uncomfortable around me."

Spike moved a little farther away from her on the bed, as if not wanting to crowd her in any way.

Her mind went through her memories of him, focusing on the moments when he'd disappeared even when he was right in front of her. "So this is what you hide. This is what you don't talk about."

"Yes. I… Mad, I didn't mention it to you in the beginning because I figured we were just friends. But then things got complicated. I was going to tell you, I swear. Especially after I decided…"

"What?"

"That I wanted to see you again. Often."

She looked at him for a long time, then reached out for his hand. He seemed surprised that she would want to touch him, his eyes widening.

As their fingers intertwined she said, "I wanted that, too. I want that."

His brows shot up. "Even though you know?"

"Yes. I can't pretend that I'm not shocked. I am. But I'm not frightened of you. And I'm not going to stop…" Now that she was fully awake she found it hard to say the *L* word. "I still want to see you."

"Are you sure?" He bent down and kissed her hand, squeezing it tight. "Because I figured…with the way you lost your mother, this would be especially difficult for you to accept."

She frowned. "The way I lost my…what does my mother dying of cancer have to do with your having been to prison?"

Spike's face registered undiluted shock. Like the kind people showed at traffic accidents. "Excuse me?"

"My mother died of cancer. So why should your past be hard to accept because of that?"

"What?"

"I… Why are you so surprised by this?"

He cursed and then those yellow eyes narrowed until they were slits. "You have no idea what… Holy hell."

Holy hell was right, she thought. Spike was truly furious. And trying very hard not to show it.

"How did you think she died?" Mad asked.

"It doesn't matter—"

She cut him right off. "Michael Moriarty, so help me God, you better not withhold anything from me anymore. If you and I are going to be together in some way, we are starting a no-hiding rule right now. Either you are totally up front with me or you and I are going nowhere fast."

His brows lifted. Then he smiled a little. "Okay. I…ah, all right. You know, I kind of like it when you order me around."

"Good. Get used to it. If I can handle the boys on the crew, I can handle you. Now spill it."

He kissed her quick and hard. Then got serious.

"Richard told me that your mother had died in the course of a violent felony. He said he'd looked into my background and gone to you as soon as he found out about my past. Maintained you'd left because you didn't want to see me anymore. That's why when I came to you in Newport, I was so surprised you thought I'd been with Amelia."

"What a...bastard," she said, appalled. That Richard could lie...about her mother? Could manipulate Spike and her like this?

"Mad, what are you thinking right now?"

Clearly, she'd been quiet for awhile. "I...I stood up for him at the board meeting this afternoon. Backed his acquisition proposal because it was the correct business thing to do. Even told him he was the right man for the CEO job because he was and is good in that role. But after this..." She shook her head. "Someone who can be that unethical, should not be running any kind of company."

No, Richard definitely had to go. And not in retaliation for what he'd done to her and Spike, although she was going to give the man plenty of hell for that. Richard had to go because ethics in one's personal life were indistinguishable from ethics in one's business life.

And she would get him out. With the amount of shares under her control, she would find a way to make the change. And she was willing to bet Sean and Mick would help her.

She refocused on Spike. And smiled as she noted that he hadn't let go of her hand.

"So where does this leave us?" she asked.

He hesitated. "Well, all things considering...I'd say we're in love." He leaned in close and punctuated his sentences with kisses. "Yeah. Definitely. Because I love you. You love me. So, we're in love."

"We're in love?" She almost couldn't believe it.

"Yeah. We are."

She wrapped her arms around him and held on tight.

"But Mad, about the sailing."

She braced herself, wondering what she would do if he said he wanted her to give up her sport. "What about it?"

"Don't worry, I wouldn't dream of asking you to stop racing." As she relaxed and smiled, he said, "But I think it would be great if you…didn't drive yourself too hard. You know, with the working out stuff and the dieting. I love your body the way it is now, but I think I'd love it even more if you…ah, that is I wish you would…"

She kissed him to reassure him. "I've already started changing things. I've been thinking lately that someday, I might want to have kids. So I need to begin getting ready even now."

He cut her off with his lips as if he couldn't control the impulse. "I want to have babies with you. Lots of babies."

She grinned at the possessive tone in his voice. "Do you now?"

"Yes…" But then he cursed and winced. "Actually… there's something else. And we're under that no-hiding rule, aren't we?"

"We sure are."

"Okay…well, I want to marry you. Tomorrow. Tonight. Right now." He blew out his breath. "There. I said it. Yes, I know we haven't known each other long—"

This time she was the one cutting him off with a kiss. "You know what? I think it's a great idea."

"You do?"

She smiled up at him. "I do."

Epilogue

Spike and Mad said their official *I do's* two weeks later in a small civil ceremony at the Saranac Lake courthouse. The rings they exchanged were plain platinum, his a little wider, hers a little thinner. Their honeymoon was spent on a sailing yacht. Mad showed Spike how to set and stay a nautical course. Spike showed Mad how to make home-made risotto.

Unfortunately, they ended up miles off in the wrong direction. And Mad's risotto had the consistency of runny oatmeal and tasted like spackle. Both of them, however, were perfectly happy with the results. But then again, true love doesn't care about the minor details of life, like miles lost and time wasted getting back on course. And it is fed by things other than competence in the kitchen.

Love thrives where there is warmth in the heart for another. And now that they've found each other, Spike and Mad are always warm.

* * * * *

Happily ever after is just the beginning...

Turn the page for a sneak preview of
DANCING ON SUNDAY AFTERNOONS
by
Linda Cardillo

Harlequin Everlasting—Every great love
has a story to tell. ™
A brand-new line from Harlequin Books
launching this February!

Prologue

Giulia D'Orazio
1983

I had two husbands—Paolo and Salvatore.

Salvatore and I were married for thirty-two years. I still live in the house he bought for us; I still sleep in our bed. All around me are the signs of our life together. My bedroom window looks out over the garden he planted. In the middle of the city, he coaxed tomatoes, peppers, zucchini—even grapes for his wine—out of the ground. On weekends, he used to drive up to his cousin's farm in Waterbury and bring back manure. In the winter, he wrapped the peach tree and the fig tree with rags and black rubber hoses against the cold, his massive, coarse hands gentling those trees as if they were his fragile-skinned babies. My neighbor, Dominic Grazza, does that for me now. My boys have no time for the garden.

In the front of the house, Salvatore planted roses. The roses I take care of myself. They are giant, cream-colored, fragrant. In the afternoons, I like to sit out on the porch with my coffee, protected from the eyes of the neighborhood by that curtain of flowers.

Salvatore died in this house thirty-five years ago. In the last months, he lay on the sofa in the parlor so he could be in the middle of everything. Except for the two oldest boys, all the children were still at home and we ate together every evening. Salvatore could see the dining room table from the sofa, and he could hear everything that was said. "I'm not dead, yet," he told me. "I want to know what's going on."

When my first grandchild, Cara, was born, we brought her to him, and he held her on his chest, stroking her tiny head. Sometimes they fell asleep together.

Over on the radiator cover in the corner of the parlor is the portrait Salvatore and I had taken on our twenty-fifth anniversary. This brooch I'm wearing today, with the diamonds—I'm wearing it in the photograph also—Salvatore gave it to me that day. Upstairs on my dresser is a jewelry box filled with necklaces and bracelets and earrings. All from Salvatore.

I am surrounded by the things Salvatore gave me, or did for me. But, God forgive me, as I lie alone now in my bed, it is Paolo I remember.

Paolo left me nothing. Nothing, that is, that my family, especially my sisters, thought had any value. No house. No diamonds. Not even a photograph.

But after he was gone, and I could catch my breath from

the pain, I knew that I still had something. In the middle of the night, I sat alone and held them in my hands, reading the words over and over until I heard his voice in my head. I had Paolo's letters.

* * * * *

Be sure to look for
DANCING ON SUNDAY AFTERNOONS
available January 30, 2007.

And look, too, for our other Everlasting title available,
FALL FROM GRACE by Kristi Gold.

FALL FROM GRACE is a deeply emotional story
of what a long-term love really means.
As Jack and Anne Morgan discover, marriage vows
can be broken—but they can be mended, too.
And the memories of their marriage
have an unexpected power to bring back a love
that never really left....

HARLEQUIN *Romance*.

What a month!

In February watch for

Rancher and Protector
Part of the Western Weddings miniseries
BY JUDY CHRISTENBERRY

The Boss's Pregnancy Proposal
BY RAYE MORGAN

Also in February, expect
MORE of what you love
as the Harlequin Romance line
increases to six titles per month.

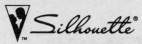

This February...

Catch NASCAR Superstar **Carl Edwards** *in*

SPEED DATING!

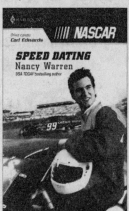

Kendall assesses risk for a living—
so she's the last person you'd
expect to see on the arm of a
race-car driver who thrives on the
unpredictable. But when a bizarre
turn of events—and NASCAR
hotshot Dylan Hargreave—inspire
her to trade in her ever-so-structured
existence for "life in the fast lane"
she starts to feel she might be
on to something!

HARLEQUIN®

Super Romance®

Is it really possible to find true love
when you're single…with kids?

Introducing an exciting new five-book miniseries,

SINGLES...WITH KIDS

When Margo almost loses her bistro…and custody of
her children…she realizes a real family is about more
than owning a pretty house and being a perfect mother.
And then there's the new man in her life, Robert…
Like the other single parents in her support group, she
has to make sure he wants the whole package.

Starting in February 2007 with

LOVE AND THE SINGLE MOM

by C.J. Carmichael

(Harlequin Superromance #1398)

ALSO WATCH FOR:

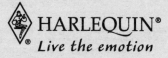

HARLEQUIN®
Live the emotion

REQUEST YOUR FREE BOOKS!
2 FREE NOVELS PLUS 2 FREE GIFTS!

Silhouette®

SPECIAL EDITION®

Life, Love and Family!

YES! Please send me 2 FREE Silhouette Special Edition® novels and my 2 FREE gifts. After receiving them, if I don't wish to receive any more books, I can return the shipping statement marked "cancel." If I don't cancel, I will receive 6 brand-new novels every month and be billed just $4.24 per book in the U.S., or $4.99 per book in Canada, plus 25¢ shipping and handling per book and applicable taxes, if any*. That's a savings of at least 15% off the cover price! I understand that accepting the 2 free books and gifts places me under no obligation to buy anything. I can always return a shipment and cancel at any time. Even if I never buy another book from Silhouette, the two free books and gifts are mine to keep forever.

235 SDN EEYU   335 SDN EEY6

Name	(PLEASE PRINT)	
Address		Apt.
City	State/Prov.	Zip/Postal Code

Signature (if under 18, a parent or guardian must sign)

Mail to the **Silhouette Reader Service™:**
IN U.S.A.: P.O. Box 1867, Buffalo, NY 14240-1867
IN CANADA: P.O. Box 609, Fort Erie, Ontario L2A 5X3

Not valid to current Silhouette Special Edition subscribers.

Want to try two free books from another line?
Call 1-800-873-8635 or visit www.morefreebooks.com.

* Terms and prices subject to change without notice. NY residents add applicable sales tax. Canadian residents will be charged applicable provincial taxes and GST. This offer is limited to one order per household. All orders subject to approval. Credit or debit balances in a customer's account(s) may be offset by any other outstanding balance owed by or to the customer. Please allow 4 to 6 weeks for delivery.

Your Privacy: Silhouette is committed to protecting your privacy. Our Privacy Policy is available online at www.eHarlequin.com or upon request from the Reader Service. From time to time we make our lists of customers available to reputable firms who may have a product or service of interest to you. If you would prefer we not share your name and address, please check here. ☐

SSE07

Silhouette®

COMING NEXT MONTH

SPECIAL EDITION

SSECNM0107